He towered over her like a god

A god with midnight-black hair and a khaki bush jacket and trousers that fitted snugly over his powerful body. Sara sighed. Help had come after all.

"I'm hurt," she whispered. "I never thought anyone would come."

He looked down at her and dropped to one knee, his dark eyes piercingly intent on her pale face. "Sara." His voice was low, but he said her name forcefully, ordering her back to full consciousness.

The effect was electric. "You!" she cried. She tried to move, but his hand fell hard on her, forbidding any movement. "No! Oh, no!"

And she slid back into unconsciousness, escaping him in the only way possible.

PATRICIA WILSON used to live in Yorkshire, England, but with her children all grown up, she decided to give up her teaching position there and accompany her husband on an extended trip to Spain. Their travels are providing her with plenty of inspiration for her romance writing.

Books by Patricia Wilson

HARLEQUIN PRESENTS

HARLEQUIN ROMANCE

PATRICIA WILSON

when the gods choose

Harlequin Books

TORONTO • NEW YORK • LONDON
AMSTERDAM • PARIS • SYDNEY • HAMBURG
STOCKHOLM • ATHENS • TOKYO • MILAN

Harlequin Presents first edition August 1989
ISBN 0-373-11198-3

Original hardcover edition published in 1988
by Mills & Boon Limited

CHAPTER ONE

SARA felt a wave of unease when she saw the extent of the glittering splendour of the ball at the Mexican Trade Mission. She hadn't quite expected this when she had talked John Culver into bringing her.

It had taken a lot of self-discipline to even approach him. He had always set her teeth on edge, and he certainly hadn't altered since the days when she had known him at her grandmother's house. He was here now, bordering on the effete or trying to be, all a studied pose as he pretended to be uninterested in her reason for being here, stopping to gossip with everyone his eye fell upon.

Sara began to simmer quietly. She was already annoyed that she had been forced to tell him some of her reasons for begging this favour, and she could well do without this deliberate lagging behind. She was not here for pleasure. The dress and accessories she had been obliged to buy had set her holiday savings back by three months at least, and she intended to get the proper use out of them at once. The chances of her ever being at a function like this again were infinitesimal, certainly not if she could help it!

'All right, old girl?'

He came alongside and Sara took his arm in a no-nonsense grip that brought a slightly pained expression to his face. If he was pretending to be the Scarlet Pimpernel, there was no way she was going to assist him! To the world he was Sir John Culver, a rising star at the Foreign Office, but to her grandmother he had been

'That fool, Johnny!' and though it grieved her to agree with her grandmother in any way, she had to admit that that was exactly how she thought of him.

'Interesting, isn't it?' he murmured, looking round the splendid room, the subtle hint of the barbaric in the brilliant wall hangings, the discreetly placed artefacts. 'Just borderin' on the scary! Hardly think you were in London. Interesting though, I mean in view of your connections with Mexico...'

He knew full well that she had no connections with Mexico at all, except for an absentee father. It was typical of his little bursts of childish spite, and his attitude did nothing to endear him to her, but interest was beginning to bubble up inside. She tightened her grip. He was not going to be allowed to sidetrack now.

'Which one is Señor Carreras?' Sara said eagerly, keeping him determinedly to the task in hand. At great pains to make sure that Sara did not change her mind about accompanying him, he had assured her that there would be a man here tonight who knew the hinterland of Mexico better than anyone alive.

'Wouldn't recognise him if he sprang at me!' he said infuriatingly. 'But there's a Señor Perez, Head of the Trade Mission. He'll point Carreras out. I happen to know that's why many people are here tonight, to try and talk to Carreras,' he added, with his annoying little habit of 'I know a secret', and Sara bit her lip in vexation. She had not thought that she would have to queue up to get the great man's attention.

'You're sure he acts as a guide?' she said severely.

'Oh, I expect so. He's supposed to know Mexico better than anyone.' He was back into his usual vague character, and Sara stifled the momentary twinge of unease. John had suggested Carreras when she had talked to him;

now it seemed he was not at all sure. Still, it mattered not one bit. Anyone who knew Mexico would do. If this man Carreras was here, then all she needed from John was an introduction. She could do the rest herself. If Carreras refused, there would be someone else. If she could arrange for a guide while she was still in England, William was more likely to give her daring idea his blessing. At the moment he was furious.

The dress she wore was jade green, a light, wispy organza that floated around her as she walked, the sort of dress she had dreamed of but had never had in her life before. She had never been able to afford anything like it, and she could not afford it now, but this was so very important to her that she had stifled the pangs of conscience and bought it, together with gold sandals and evening bag. She had to make a good impression, and she could rely on John Culver for one thing at least— he was pushy! Having assured her that Carreras was important, he would see to it that she met him, if only to prove to her how important he was himself.

'Ah! There, look!' John brightened up and pointed across the room. 'There's Señor Perez. We'll have a word, and then we'll ask after Carreras.'

All the Mexicans were beautifully dressed, she noticed, especially the tall man talking to Señor Perez, the head of the Trade Mission. There was wealth there; it showed in the man's clothes, his confident stance, the smoothly expensive haircut. For some reason or other, her eyes stayed on him, and to her consternation he suddenly turned, as if he felt her appraisal.

It was like being struck by lightning, and for a second every bit of breath seemed to leave her body as wave after wave of vivid awareness swept over her. They were still some distance apart, and yet it seemed that she was staring into two black and glittering eyes from only inches away. The room, the noise, the music all faded, and only that face, those eyes, were real.

His lean, dark face showed no emotion. There was just the hypnotic black gaze, the rapt attention, the way that his eyes never left hers. Men had looked at her before, and she knew that her hair was an attraction in itself and that tonight, against the jade green of the dress, it shone with a light of its own, tawny as autumn leaves. But no man had ever looked at her in quite the same way. This was no sexual appraisal, no quick, skimming glance over her slender figure, only the vivid intensity of his eyes locking with hers, an aloof assessment in the dark, aristocratic face, an irritated awareness in the tall, superbly masculine frame.

She could not look away, could not snap out of the breathless feeling, and her face flooded with colour as he frowned and turned deliberately away. Whoever he was, he had not liked her staring at him. His cold re- action to it had quite unnerved her, and her hand on John's arm was not now so firm and determined. She would rather not go to meet Señor Perez at this minute. She had plenty of time to wait until his haughty friend had gone.

John, though, had come out of his lethargic role and made a beeline forward, taking her along forcefully. Being Foreign Office, he knew most people, and she was introduced to the kindly-looking man who was leading this delegation, forcing herself to turn to face him, well aware that dark, disapproving eyes watched her.

'Miss Sara Lawrence,' John Culver was saying when she at last returned to some semblance of reality. 'Her father is the archaeologist, Hector Lawrence. You probably know him?' he added with that curiously bored air that he had cultivated over the years.

'I do not actually know him, *señorita*, but I certainly know of him; who in Mexico does not? He has been in—seclusion for some years now, however. Did he return to England, then, after all?'

'No, Sara intends to go out to Mexico and find him,' John Culver drawled, offering one of the titbits of information that Sara had been forced to give him.

'You will be welcome in my country, Señorita Lawrence. May I meanwhile introduce my friend and fellow countryman, Señor Jaime Carreras—he also has a great interest in our country's past.'

Sara's heart sank like a stone. *This* man was Carreras! Not a very auspicious beginning, but she would have to try. There was no putting off the inevitable, and Sara turned back to the tall Mexican whose eyes were still intently on her face.

'Señorita Lawrence.' He bowed slightly and took her hand, his eyes never leaving hers, and Sara felt the colour flare over her face at the look in those eyes. Either he disliked English women, or he had suspected her of eyeing him openly. She could well believe that his aristocratic mind would find that distasteful.

He made no attempt to speak, and John took the opportunity to once again take charge of the conversation.

'Actually, Señor Carreras,' he confided with a light laugh, 'I strongly suspect that the only reason that Sara consented to be my partner this evening was in the hope of meeting you. She wants a guide, and I rather think that she's hoping to persuade you to fill the role.'

She could have killed John! She had just decided that, however urgent her need, she would ask no favours of this man. Whatever he had been thinking when he had met her eyes across the room, John had now confirmed.

'A guide, *señorita*?' His voice was smokily soft and faintly sardonic, making her colour flare yet again. 'If you require a safari around this beautiful but cold city, then I can only tell you that I would have both of us lost within minutes. I am sure that Sir John knows London far better than I do.'

He was looking at her with a disdainful amusement that made her temper flare. He had deliberately misunderstood, and she couldn't decide who annoyed her most—John or this tall, arrogant Mexican.

'I want to find my father, Señor Carreras. I need a guide in Mexico, not here.'

She looked at him angrily and he instantly repaid her in kind.

'You have taken a very long time to look for him, *señorita*. To my certain knowledge, he has been alone in the interior for fifteen years. I doubt very much if you would even recognise him.'

Her face paled at this remark, which was clearly a reprimand, but she made herself face him.

'Do you know my father, Señor Carreras?' she asked coldly, her slim hands clenched at her sides.

'No, *señorita*, I do not, not now. Once I did. He filled me with the desire to follow in his footsteps. I doubt very much whether anyone knows him now other than the Indians of the village where he has made his home. A man without friends and family often turns to unlikely companions for comfort. It would have been better had he been looked for and brought back to his own country many years ago. Perhaps now that his family have belatedly begun to seek him, he will not wish to come.'

Sara was stunned by the antagonism and the arrogant assurance in his voice. She had not then mistaken the way he had looked at her when she had come across the room—dislike at first sight! Or maybe he had somehow already known who she was and why she was here. Certainly she had never met anyone like this man before, and he seemed to imagine that he could speak to her as he wished. Even John was stunned into silence, and Señor Perez was looking decidedly embarrassed.

'That is entirely up to him, Señor Carreras.' Her voice was shaking with anger, and his eyes moved to her clenched hands with a sort of wry satisfaction. 'I am not looking for him with even the vaguest intention of bringing him home. In fact, he has no home. I have news for him, that's all.'

'Sara's father has been left a whole heap of money!' John Culver's voice struck up, as he treacherously imparted the last bit of information that he had. 'If he doesn't come soon, the whole lot goes to someone else. That's why Sara has to find him.'

'I see!' The dark eyes looked down at her scathingly, and she could just tell what he was thinking. 'It is not then, *señorita*, for sentimental reasons?'

'I very much doubt if you *do* see, Señor Carreras,' she said quietly, with no warmth in her deep blue eyes. 'And I am not sentimental. However, as you are clearly not a guide...'

She started to turn away, but his voice stopped her. 'I could be the best guide that there is, *señorita*, but I do not act as a guide in any capacity, paid or unpaid!' There was a cold disdain on his face, and Sara was grateful for the intervention of the other Mexican.

'Señor Carreras is not in fact a guide at all, Señorita Lawrence,' he said with a pleasantry that showed why he had the job that he did so well. 'It is true that he knows the hinterland of my country better than any man alive, but the work he does there is purely on an honorary basis. The time he gives is his own, and he neither expects nor receives any recompense, except the grateful thanks of his government. Señor Carreras is a merchant banker, *señorita*, and more often than not the work that he does among the Indians is funded from his own resources.'

Sara felt new waves of feeling now, the major one being acute embarrassment, a feeling that even outweighed her desire to turn on John and beat him. Even so, it had not been as unforgivable a sin as Señor Carreras' sharp tone to her. He had no right to speak to her as he had done, and her face was hot but well controlled when she turned to him.

'I'm sorry, Señor Carreras.' Her apology was not delivered with any charm. 'It appears that I will have to look elsewhere for a guide.'

'I would advise, *señorita*, that your wisest course of action would be to abandon the whole idea of a trip to find your father,' he said with studied coldness. 'The country where he is believed to be is not easy to travel, and it is very remote, dangerous for a woman, even a Mexican woman,' he added, with a look that told her she was undoubtedly soft all through. 'Perhaps a message would do just as well?'

'I very much doubt it, Señor Carreras,' Sara said, matching his cold tones but hearing herself how temper coloured her voice. 'There is a time factor involved.'

'We have a postal service which finally gets to all parts of the country, *señorita*,' he informed her with arrogantly inclined head, the glittering dark eyes looking down at her. 'We do not rely upon a runner with a cleft stick.'

'I'm sure that you don't, *señor*,' she said, fighting hard not to slap him. 'However, I intend to take the message myself.'

'You would be more at home in Acapulco, Señorita Lawrence,' he taunted, his eyes at last skimming her figure and the beauty of her expensive dress.

It was more than enough. With a muttered goodbye, Sara escaped, feeling the inclination to break into a run and to snatch her arm away from John when he caught up with her. The other Mexican had been called away before these final exchanges and she was glad. He was too pleasant a man to be embarrassed by someone like Señor Carreras. As to John Culver, she was furious with him!

'Why did you let me believe that that man would be helpful?' she stormed quietly when they were dancing.

'I honestly thought that he would be,' he protested. 'At the very least, I thought he would show interest. He must know exactly where your father is. In fact, I'll tell you this much, if Carreras doesn't know, then nobody knows. You can hardly blame me that he took an instant dislike to you!'

'No, that's true,' Sara agreed fairly. 'Never mind, John. Thanks for bringing me. Perhaps I'll get somebody else to help while I'm here.'

'I wouldn't think so, Sara,' he said with every sign of genuine regret. 'If Carreras frowns then you are definitely *persona non grata*. You heard that Carreras is a merchant banker—in fact, he's a lot more than that. To most people he's almost Mr Mexico. He's welcome in all circles, right to the very top. His word counts. If he shook his head, you wouldn't even get a permit to go into the country.'

'Nobody's that powerful!' Sara protested, looking up at him.

'Oh, yes, they are, m'dear,' he assured her, and one quick, anxious glance at Señor Carreras convinced her. He was surrounded by the most important-looking men, the most glittering ladies, all hanging on to his words. Frighteningly though, his eyes were on her, dark and unfathomable, filling her with a gathering dread that almost outweighed her anger.

She tore her eyes away and concentrated on John and the people he knew, throwing herself into the spirit of things, determined to get the best out of this. The dress, after all, had been a sheer waste of money. She had been humiliated, chastised and almost frightened. There must be somebody here, though, who could help, somebody who knew a good, reputable guide.

John seemed to be very contrite and anxious to help as much as he could, quite forgetting his brittle ways as he guided her from one person to the next. It was quite useless, though. All voices directed her back to Carreras, and all eyes turned rather worriedly to him at the slightest suggestion that there could be anyone who knew Mexico as well.

Wherever she went his eyes seemed to follow her, and it was like waiting for fate to catch up with her. He was determined for some reason that she should not go to find her father, and she knew that he would do something. Deep inside she was holding her breath, partly from frustration and partly from sheer worry. Why he should even take any notice, she could not think.

He did nothing, though, until they were almost ready to leave, and then, as she was dancing with John, she was aware of him behind her, even though she never turned.

'You will allow me this dance, I am sure.' The smoky voice, softly accented, was almost in her ear, and every muscle in her body tightened as he calmly extricated her from John's arms and swept her off across the crowded floor.

'It would have been perfectly easy to send me a message if you wanted to speak to me, Señor Carreras,' she said as firmly as she could, deliberately turning her head away, too scared if she could admit it to look at him. His eyes on her had seemed to be trying to rob her of any will and now in his arms she realised what a battle she had on her hands.

'I did not wish to send you a message, *señorita*,' he said softly and firmly. 'Messages have a way of being heard by those that are not concerned with them. This matter concerns you and me alone.'

'You mean that you're going to guide me to my father?' Sara asked, knowing as she said it that the very thought alarmed her.

'I mean nothing of the sort, Señorita Lawrence!' he snapped. 'I have no intention of either guiding you to your father or of allowing anyone else to do so. He has been alone for many years. Leave him in peace with his people!'

'Your people, you mean, Señor Carreras! My father is English!'

'What a great pity that your family did not realise that many years ago!' he grated, his hands tightening harshly on her. 'In any case, I did not come here to exchange insults with you. I wish you to know that I will not permit you to go now and disturb him!'

'You *own* Mexico, Señor Carreras?' Sara asked sarcastically, and he looked down his straight nose at her, his eyes glitteringly black.

'Not quite, *señorita*!' he rasped. 'I do have a certain power there, however, and complete power here tonight. There is no person at this gathering who would even lift a finger to help you unless I gave a nod of approval.'

'Instead you've been carefully watching me and quietly shaking your head!' Sara flared. 'I'm astounded at the interest you're showing in someone so lowly as myself! Try to ignore me, *señor*, and try to mind your own business!'

'I will gladly ignore you when you give up this idiotic adventure!' he said coldly. 'As to my interest, I remember your father, *señorita*, and I do not like greed!'

'It's amazing how the rich can discount money!' Sara scoffed. 'I shall do exactly as I please!'

'Not while I have my eye on you!' he said scathingly. 'The rabbit may struggle in the trap, but he is trapped just the same!'

'I'm not trapped!' Sara snapped, glaring at him, and he smiled down in amusement.

'Not until you arrive in Mexico, *señorita*,' he said with a sinister quiet. 'There you will find that all roads lead to Carreras.'

'When I arrive, Señor Carreras, and I *shall* arrive, you won't even know that I'm there. It's not a country that I look forward to seeing, but I know that it's big!'

'Not big enough to hide in, *señorita*,' he assured her calmly. 'You will need papers, documents, permission; all the information I ever need is passed to me as soon as I require it. You cannot sneak into my country as a thief!'

'I have no wish to take even the tiniest grain of Mexican soil!' Sara ground out. 'I have a lifetime of hatred for your country. I want to find my father and then get out as fast as possible. Don't be afraid, *señor*, I won't try to remove your famous visitor!'

'He is famous no more,' the Mexican said quietly. 'Leave an old man in peace and pursue your fortunes elsewhere. I'm sure a girl with your—talents will not be waiting long for good fortune.'

His eyes flared over her insolently, and she tensed to draw back and slap the irritating, haughty face, but he caught her wrist with fingers like steel.

'I would not advise it, *señorita*,' he cautioned softly, his black eyes narrowed. 'I may take reprisals that you would not welcome at all. Certainly I would not just accept a blow gratefully!'

There was a compelling glow in the dark eyes, a glitter of light deep in their black depths, and she was almost hysterically glad when John intervened.

'I think we should be going, Sara!' he said peevishly. 'I did promise William that I'd get you back fairly early, and it's gone midnight. He'll never sleep until you're there.'

Sara looked up at the tall Mexican, and was in time to see his stunned look change to disgust as John stalked off to get her wrap.

'Be warned, *señorita*,' he said tightly. 'Forget your search. The country you are proposing to visit is wild and dangerous. There are guides, but for a woman alone, the idea is preposterous!'

'I make up my own mind, Señor Carreras,' she said coolly, feeling less menaced now that she was about to leave. 'It is a very long time since anyone told me what to do!'

'It is advice only, *señorita*!'

'Then you won't mind if I ignore it, will you? I really must go now. John is quite right. William will be champing at the bit!'

'Your horse, *señorita*?' He looked down at her scornfully and she managed a scathing look of her own.

'William is the man in my life, *señor*!'

'Your husband?' He glowered down at her and she managed a laugh, her small, white, even teeth perfect against the coral of her lips.

'No such thing, Señor Carreras. We merely live together!'

He didn't look particularly surprised. 'He lends you out for the evening, *señorita*? Is he not consumed with jealousy to know that you are out with Sir John, dancing with other men?'

'We live our own separate lives. It's a good arrangement,' Sara said tartly, 'but I really don't like to worry him. Goodnight, Señor Carreras.'

He did not reply, and she turned at the door for a last look at him. She knew she would never see him again and she was glad of that but, even so, it was hurtful in a strange sort of way. Nobody had ever disliked her on sight before.

She could understand his disdain when he thought she was merely hunting for money, but he had disliked her even before she had opened her mouth. Irritation had flared across his face almost as soon as he had seen her.

Now, he thought that she was living with a man, and she had taken great pleasure in confirming that belief. Living with William! Her lips curved into a smile of amusement. If William had heard the mighty *señor* tonight, he would have taken his stick to him! He would probably take it to her too when she got home and confessed where she had been. Her cousin William disapproved of this almost as much as Señor Carreras did, but for entirely different reasons. William knew that, far from chasing wealth, she was trying to make sure that wealth did not force itself upon her. Not this wealth! Not her grandmother's money!

It was a bitterly cold evening, but the chill she felt was deep inside as she thought of her grandmother and her mother. She would never see Señor Jaime Carreras again, and she wished she had never heard of Mexico.

'Arrogant chap!' John muttered bad-temperedly, and she could only agree. But Carreras had been more than that. He had frightened her into thinking that she would not get into Mexico, and she *had* to! There was a promise to keep. Somehow, she could go there, and time was short.

Sara sat back in the warmth of John's car and thought back to that morning when she had inherited this problem. The letter had been there when she had come downstairs to breakfast, and William had been sitting at the table, observing it sombrely.

'Letter from your grandmother's solicitors, by the look of it,' he informed her with a quizzical look. 'You'll have to open it and face the facts,' he added when she simply poured her tea, ignoring the long white envelope.

William could be very firm when he wanted, and Sara looked at him defiantly for only a second longer before reaching out her slim hand and taking the envelope from the table.

'What the hell! It's only a piece of paper! It can't leap up and bite me!'

'Sensible girl,' William encouraged quietly, his good-natured face beaming at her with that fatherly expression he reserved for his most favoured pupils.

She smiled across at him and opened the letter, but her courage failed her at the first line.

'As you were not present at the reading of the will, we feel it essential that you are acquainted with the following facts...'

'Read it, William! I can't!'

She pushed the letter across and he gave her one of his wry looks before reading it through in silence as she sipped anxiously at her tea, asking herself why she should be getting so desperate about a mere letter. There was nothing that could touch her, nothing that could hurt her again—she was with William!

She had always been close to her cousin William, and after her mother had died it was the most natural thing in the world that they should have pooled their resources and taken this little house. William taught at the local school, and Sara could get a train from here to London with no difficulty, to be at her desk in the bank in good time. They were company for each other and quite content to leave things as they were.

They were both bruised by life in their separate ways. William had been lame from birth—not any severe disfigurement, simply one leg slightly shorter than the other, which meant that he had to use a stick constantly. He was a handsome man, blessed by the family colouring: the wild, tawny hair and the deep blue eyes. His driving ambition was to open a school of his own, a very special school for handicapped children.

Sara was devoted to William. She felt safe with him. He never tried to alter her or crush her sparkling nature. The woman who had tried that was gone now.

'Do you want the lot, or a brief résumé?' William asked softly as he finished reading.

'Briefly, please.' Sara's hands gripped her cup tightly, her eyes intent on his face.

'Briefly then, and in normal as opposed to legal terms, the whole of your grandmother's estate goes to your father. If he should still be missing six months from the dating of this letter, he will be presumed dead, as he has been missing for so long. In this event, the lot comes to you. That's it in a nutshell.'

'No!' Sara leapt to her feet, her face white and furious. 'She can't do this to me! She knew very well how I felt! It's all to spite Mother!'

'Sara, love, they're both *dead*! Are you suggesting that there's a grudge that goes on after death? Be fair! You're the only surviving relative. If your father is dead, then naturally you get the lot.'

'He's not dead!' Sara exclaimed bitterly, beginning to pace restlessly about. 'He's where he's been for the last twenty years, in his wretched Mexico, doing what he wants to do with no thought for either mother or me!'

'He hasn't been heard of for years,' William reminded her quietly. 'With a man who was once so famous, it's reasonable to suppose that he's no longer alive.'

'Nothing is reasonable with him!' Sara stormed, her deep blue eyes flashing. 'Was it reasonable to go off and leave his wife and baby with his mother? Was it reasonable to never come back? He wasn't dead then! He was in all the papers. My mother kept the cuttings!'

'I can understand her bitterness, Sara, but she passed it on to you. Nobody should have that kind of legacy.'

'I promised, I vowed when she was dying that I would never, ever have one penny of Grandmother's money!'

'It was a promise she had no right to extract from you, Sara. Bitterness can turn somebody into a person who's unrecognisable. It's corrosive. It eats away at the soul.'

'We only had each other!' Her eyes were filled with tears now, bitter tears, and he looked at her evenly.

'Oddly enough, old thing, I always thought that you had me,' he reminded her quietly, and it melted her anger instantly.

'Oh, William! I'm sorry!'

'Humble apologies accepted. Get your breakfast or you'll miss the train,' he advised with a grin.

'I have it!' Her sudden exclamation a few seconds later had William's eyes intently on her again. 'I'll go out to Mexico and get my father! I'll make him come and accept the money! At the very least, I'll get any necessary signatures!' She smiled triumphantly at William, and he looked at her as if she was hopelessly mad.

'Sheer nonsense! You have five minutes to get ready or you'll miss that train!'

William was against it. The arrogant Señor Carreras was against it. But Sara knew that it had to be done.

'What—er—plans have you now, Sara?' John asked as he drew up to her house. 'I mean, now that Carreras has scotched that one?'

'I don't know, John.' She smiled briefly, tired and very disturbed by what could only be described as a catastrophic evening.

'If I think of anything, I'll be in touch,' he said helpfully. 'Somehow or other we'll have to get you to Mexico and get a guide. Dreadful thought that you should lose all that money! Not to worry, old thing, I'm sure you'll get the cash!'

'Yes, I'll have to get there,' she said brightly as she got out. As to the having the money, he only had part of the story; he was as ignorant of the truth as Carreras.

'Over my dead body!' she muttered, going inside, and out of the bitterly cold night.

William was in bed and Sara went quietly to her room. This evening's little débâcle she would keep to herself; time enough to tell William when she had got herself a guide. Nothing would stop her from doing that!

CHAPTER TWO

THE DAY after the ball, the bitter cold continued, and Sara knew there would soon be snow. It was a grey, miserable day, matching exactly how she felt inside. That morning she had had cross words with William, and they had both gone to their separate jobs without making it up at all. She hated to quarrel with him. He was more than a cousin to her, he was her lifelong friend, and the depression she felt was hard to shrug off; but he would not give ground at all about her idea of going to find her father.

Last night's fiasco had depressed her, too. She had hardly slept at all. Every time she closed her eyes the image of Jaime Carreras swam into her inner vision as she built up resentment against him. She was still smarting from the cruel lash of his tongue, his arrogance rankling. He was not very easy to dismiss from her thoughts, and she writhed in annoyance as she thought of many things she could have said—the pique of hindsight!

She didn't know him, would never see him again, and it was ridiculous that she felt so affronted by his opinion of her. Of course, she could have blurted out the whole of her story! She could have told him about the powerful grandmother who had ruled both her own life and her mother's after Hector Lawrence had gone back to his real love—old ruins! How finally they had become totally dependent on her, and that she had not realised the true state of affairs until almost too late.

It was none of his business! All she had wanted was a guide, and she was prepared to pay out the last of her savings to get one. If he thought himself so important that he could stop her, then he was mistaken! He was power-mad! She tried to dismiss him from her thoughts, but he refused to go, his haughty image reinforcing her smouldering feelings of resentment towards his country.

Once again, she used John Culver, phoning him during her lunch break to see if he could find out where the delegation from Mexico were staying. She had not by any means managed to get round to them all last night. If she were to drop on one of them unexpectedly, to surprise them into giving her information or even one name, she would be quite satisfied. John rose to the occasion and in the afternoon he telephoned. They were at the Phoenix.

Four-thirty found her outside the hotel, trying to gather the courage to go in and ask for room numbers. It was almost dark and bitterly cold but, faced with the necessary evil of walking boldly in and spinning a plausible tale, she hesitated, realising that she did not have as much nerve as she had thought.

She paced about a little, rehearsing a variety of possible excuses to get in there, and the voice that spoke almost in her ear startled her into immobility.

'You are waiting for me, Señorita Lawrence?'

She spun round and found herself looking into two glittering eyes that seemed to be uncertain whether to be furiously annoyed or highly amused, as Jaime Carreras planted his tall frame in front of her and shocked her into silence. She just knew that her mouth was open!

'It is astonishing that you have succeeded in catching me!' he remarked smoothly. 'I have merely been paying a visit. Naturally, Señor Perez and I are staying at the Savoy!'

Naturally! Sara gulped down her shock and geared herself for battle.

'I am not waiting for you, Señor Carreras!' she snapped, a little of the colour coming back into her face, 'and if I caught you I would drop you rapidly, believe me!'

'Like—how do you say—a hot potato?' he enquired silkily, confounding her by his knowledge of the finer points of the English insult. 'Did you know, *señorita*, that the Mexican Trade Delegation are staying at this hotel?' he asked with a mocking inflection in his deep voice. 'Is it not astonishing that you find yourself here and I find myself encountering you outside this place?'

'I—I happen to be waiting for somebody!' Sara said quickly, having more colour in her face now than she required.

'And he is late. How frustrating for you!' he purred smoothly. 'At least while you wait, allow me to help you in some small way. To waste time is criminal!'

Before she could protest he had taken her arm in a deceptively gentle grasp; how to get into the hotel was no longer a problem, for he almost marched her to the reception desk.

'You know, I expect, that the Mexican Trade Delegation are staying here?' he enquired politely of the startled man at the desk.

'Of course, Señor Carreras!'

'Then I wish you to take a good look at this young lady,' he insisted, turning to look at Sara's bewildered face. 'She is not to be admitted to the hotel while my fellow countrymen are here. Otherwise, there will be—repercussions, you understand!'

The threat was polite and quiet, most reasonable, and it took all of three seconds before Sara's face flamed with humiliation. The man at the desk seemed to be memorising her appearance, no doubt marking her as an enemy agent, and Jaime Carreras leaned against the desk, his dark eyes laughing, his firm lips quirking with amusement as she stormed off into the gathering dusk.

She outwitted him, however. She telephoned the hotel that very evening, and had quite a pleasant conversation with a man whose strongly accented voice informed her that guides would be no problem, it could all be arranged before she even left Mexico City. The cost varied, depending upon the length of the expedition, the equipment needed and the danger involved, but it could be sorted out within an hour, no problem at all. Her glee was more because she had got the better of one tall and arrogant Mexican, than because her journey could soon begin—and she readily admitted that!

She was stunned, therefore, the next day to hear his voice in the bank a little before lunch time, but her mind sorted itself out into astonishment and embarrassment mixed with great vexation when she looked up and saw him talking to the manager. He had found out! She might have known!

'Ah, Miss Lawrence!' Mr Partridge came across to her desk and actually beamed down at her. 'You should have told me that you had a luncheon date with Señor Carreras. You could have left much earlier!'

'I—er——' Sara stared in bewilderment, acknowledging defeat as her eyes met the black and intent gaze of Jaime Carreras. If she argued here he would only make her look a fool. 'It—er—it's not quite lunch time.'

'Never mind, Miss Lawrence! Go now, by all means. Take the rest of the day off. You don't look at all well!'

She was almost bundled open-mouthed out of the bank, certain that had she tried to re-enter she would have found the doors locked against her. The man at her side was not in any way troubled by her disconcertion. He, it seemed, was intent upon bundling her into his car, a great black Mercedes that stood parked outside the bank.

'It's a no-parking zone!' she said furiously and idiotically. 'Bank security and...'

'The only thing in the bank that I wanted to steal was you,' he said evenly, almost tipping her into the warmth of the car. 'Now I have you, we will pull away and no harm done.'

'You think you can have anything, don't you?' she cried bitterly. 'You have no right to interfere with my affairs! You've made me look a fool at the bank! I...'

'That is not so,' he said quietly, pulling smoothly into the traffic. 'I have raised your prospects considerably. You are the girl who knows Carreras. The manager will be at your feet from now on, in case you report his conduct to me.'

'Money isn't everything!' she raged, clenching her hands in her lap to stop herself from attacking him. 'I'll never live this down, and I don't even know you! Mr Partridge is an—an ogre! I have problems enough without you!'

'Money is a useful commodity, so useful that you are intent upon a foolish adventure to get some yourself,' he said impatiently. 'It was not money that turned your Mr Partridge into an early Father Christmas, however—it was power.'

'And you think you have plenty of that!' Sara snapped, feeling on the edge of tears with annoyance. 'Where do you imagine you're taking me?'

'Somewhere that is quiet, so that I can talk to you!' he said irascibly. 'It is, as you pointed out, a little early for lunch, and I do not intend to suffer the embarrassment of having you shrilly chastise me in a quiet restaurant! The park would perhaps be suitable. Should you wish to behave like a virago, I will at least be able to pretend that you are not with me!'

Chastise! He had done that to her on sight! Sara felt close to explosion.

'I've been kidnapped from my place of work!' she began in a suitably calm voice, irritated beyond words that his remarks had robbed her of the liberty of yelling into his haughty ear. 'You may turn around and take me back to the bank!'

'Were I to do that,' he assured her quietly, 'I would merely wait outside for you, and no doubt you would be interrogated about this strange state of affairs by your ogre! I would have come for you earlier, but it has taken me rather a long time to discover where you were. I intend to speak to you, at length if necessary, and there is no avoiding it, *señorita*.'

There was a finality about his voice that quite robbed her of speech, a disdain towards her personal wishes that made her look at him in stunned silence. She felt, for the moment, helpless. Anyone who ever had to rely on this man's good nature would need a skin like a rhino!

'Here will do,' he remarked coolly, pulling into the side of the road. 'We can enter the park through those gates. There is no hurry, as you have the rest of the day off, and I intend to make things extremely clear to you so that we will have no further need to meet and discuss your behaviour!'

Sara took a deep breath, her face white with rage, but he totally ignored her, getting out and coming to help her out, too.

'Come!' he said, and it was all that he did say. Outside the park there were a few passers-by, and he would not want to be seen with her, of course! She set off in front of him. There were a few things that she wanted to tell him, too, and it would not be a good idea to have interested spectators, she also had pride!

There were still a few dead leaves lining the path through the park, unhappy-looking things that only emphasised the cold, grey weather, and Sara stepped out briskly, her collar turned up against the bitter wind.

'There are few people in the park,' he said into the silence, apparently imagining that he could make normal conversation until they arrived at the designated chastisement point! She shrugged, keeping her head down and marching on.

'They have more sense than to come here to get their ears frozen off!'

'You are very cold?' He stopped her, taking her arm and swinging her towards him. 'If I can be assured of your good behaviour, I will gladly take you to lunch.'

'I do not wish to eat with you!' Sara snapped, pulling her arm free from his grasp. 'I have no wish to talk to you either, but rather than have you continually haunting me, I'll stand here and talk!'

'Very well!' He was stiffly proper, and it occurred to Sara that perhaps he was offended at her refusal to eat with him; more likely, though, it was her attitude of insubordination that irritated. 'I am about to warn you for the very last time, Señorita Lawrence, of the dangers of pursuing your present course. To ask me to take you to your father was perhaps ill-advised, but at least it was safe. Many people may offer their services, few will be trustworthy. Once in the mountains, you will be helpless. That is my first objection. The other is about your father. For fifteen years he has been back in my country, and for many years now he has been quite away from civilisation. How do you imagine he is? What do you imagine he will look like? He has left his own people, his wife, his daughter and his friends. He has nothing in common with his own countrymen at all. Even his English will be rusty, unused for years. Leave him to end his days in peace!'

Sara felt a momentary pang of pity, a glimpse of a man who was utterly alone. But he had not been forced into that life, he had chosen it. Her mother had been left with no choice at all! There was her vow! Her father was a stranger, but her promise to her mother was real, still burning inside her.

'I told you once, *señor*, that you didn't understand,' she said quietly, looking up into the dark, handsome face, into the night-black eyes that watched her intently. 'I must go and find my father. There are papers that he has to sign.'

'So! Money and the search for it dictates all your actions!' he blazed, his eyes fiery with anger. 'You will disturb an old man and place your life at risk in order to gain money! It is more easily gained, *señorita*! With your looks, your figure, it should not take long at all! You are living with a man; live with someone who is wealthy!'

'Someone like you, you mean?' Sara exploded, her face flushed with anger, her blue eyes sparkling and wide.

For a second, he stood looking down at her, his body peculiarly still as his eyes flashed over her wildly angry face.

'Why not?' he murmured sardonically. 'When you are not raging you are beautiful. I have never possessed an English girl. Are you available, *señorita*?'

There was no thought behind Sara's action, only humiliation and blind rage. Her hand flashed up and delivered a stinging slap to the handsome, tormenting face of this Mexican who imagined he could stand here and insult her.

He stood perfectly still, not even rocking with the blow, and then rage such as she had never seen filled the dark eyes, and before she could move he had her tightly in his arms, his furious eyes blazing down at her.

'You were warned of reprisals!' he grated harshly. 'I will now teach you what a reprisal is!'

His mouth came down on hers, stifling her cry in a kiss that crushed her lips and jarred through her whole body. Cruelty and anger were the twin driving forces behind it, and the power of it made her feel faint and terrified. It only lasted for seconds, but when he lifted his head Sara felt degraded, locked in iron-strong arms that even now did not release her.

He looked down into her eyes, a strange light burning deep in the blackness of his gaze, and then his hand lifted, his finger tracing her lips, parting them as she stared at him in horror.

'You are very troublesome,' he said softly. 'Whatever you think of me, I am not normally cruel. There is something in you, I think, that brings out the worst in me. We are all savages at heart.'

His strong, lean fingers slid to her cheek, stroking it lightly, then cupping it in his warm palm as he lifted her face and caught her lips with his, the whole park cold and empty around them.

This time there was an unexpected gentleness, and he drew her against him so completely that the breath left Sara's body like a bird taking flight. Frightening shafts of sexual awareness pierced her as his mouth invaded hers with sensual intensity. Blind, hungry need struck through her as his hands stroked her face, the kiss seemingly endless. When he finally let her go, she was trembling all over, speechless!

Belatedly she realised that her eyes were closed, and when she opened them he was looking down at her with disdainful satisfaction, his arms no longer holding her.

'If you should ever become available, *señorita*,' he said derisively, 'telephone the Embassy. They will be able to contact me, and I have enough money for both of us.'

He stepped away, his firm lips quirking with amusement.

'Does—William kiss you like that, *señorita*?' he asked silkily, and then he turned and walked off, leaving her stunned and stranded in the park.

The following day he was in the papers, on the front page. He had been called back to Mexico, some banking crisis. She read it carefully, just to make sure he had gone, her eyes lingering on the compelling photograph that accompanied the article. An unexpected shiver flared over her skin...the kiss, *that* kiss, still too real to be brushed aside. And then she quickly folded the paper, turning his face inwards, out of her sight. She was rid of him! She could get on with her plans!

Everything was going well, almost too well. In view of William's grave doubts about the scheme, Sara felt very much on edge, but so far there had been no snags at all. She had managed a flight to Mexico with no trouble, and had even managed to charter this small and rather

tatty-looking plane to fly her out to the mountains. The
pilot was no more impressive then his plane, but it was
all she could afford, even though she had the distinct
impression that he was flying by the seat of his pants,
as it were, and not paying very much attention to any
instruments. It didn't matter. She was committed to this.
She was keeping her promise.

The plane was heading straight for the mountains,
following a dry riverbed that ran through a valley carved
here long before the land had been ruled by Spain, even
before the mighty civilisation of the Aztecs had stamped
its mark on this country. Below it was hazy, the houses
tiny doll-like buildings in a rolling landscape edged by
high mountains. Above, the sky was a bright, cloudless
blue, a backcloth of colour for the small, silvery plane.

She had not yet managed to get a guide. Someone
would volunteer closer to her destination, she had been
told, and it reminded her with a twinge of anxiety about
Jaime Carreras and his warnings three months ago.

Three months! It seemed to be much longer than that.
Now, flying closer every minute to the place where she
would hire a guide to take her to her father, she realised
that she had lived such a long time within three months.
There had been leave from the bank to arrange, papers
to get from reluctant solicitors, and above all there had
been William, who for the first time ever had actually
stormed at her, flatly refusing to be reasonable.

For a second, her face clouded with sadness, but then
she pulled herself out of it as she had pulled herself out
of things for most of her life. She was here! This was
where she wanted to be for now. This was where she
would find her father, get his signature and get the whole
business sorted out. She would make her peace with
William later, but for now she was here to make sure

that her father accepted the inheritance and that she received not one penny. Her mother's last wishes would then be granted, and maybe she would be able to forget and live her life without doubts and regrets. She would see the sort of man her father was, nail that particular ghost once and for all, and then she never wanted to even hear the name Mexico ever again in her life.

The agitated murmurings of the pilot brought her back to the present, and she looked out of the window, gasping in shock. There was nothing to see! Where minutes before she had looked up and seen the towering height of the mountains, there was now nothing. Fog surrounded the plane, fastening them into a grey shroud, filling the cabin with eerie light and changing the tone of the engines.

'How long before we land?'

She could hear the anxiety in her own voice, and had no doubt that the Mexican at the controls heard it, too.

'Soon, Señorita Lawrence. Very soon.'

She realized he was trying hard to be calm for her benefit, but there was too much anxiety in his own voice to make her feel in any way reassured.

'Can you land the plane in this fog?'

'No, *señorita*! However, do not be alarmed. These mists come rapidly in the mountains and as rapidly depart. I know where we are.'

Sara bit her lip anxiously. She also knew where they were, but that was no help. She silently berated herself for not having got a better plane when she'd been chartering one. This, though, was all she could afford. There had been the ticket out, the money for her hotel, there would be a guide to pay, and already her meagre savings would be spent. She had enough to get there and get back, and then she was broke. She would probably lose

her job, too. And all to get rid of money! It was, as
William had said, ridiculous!

'Do not be alarmed, Señorita Lawrence. The fog will
soon clear!'

He was saying it like a prayer, and Sara did what he
was doing; she stared out into the fog. He, though, was
searching for the ground, looking again for the dried
bed of the river, searching for some landmark like a pilot
of some old plane when flight was new. No doubt his
instruments were unusable, or unreadable to him! Sara
was staring ahead, her mind on the terrifying proximity
of the mountains, expecting at any second to see them
rearing out of the blanket of fog to invite the flimsy craft
to its doom.

Suddenly the fog cleared; not totally, but well enough
to give them some warning of their fate. They were not
near the mountains, they were *in* the mountains! They
were flying, by some miracle, between the sheer, harsh
walls of rock, the small plane seeming to have guided
itself into this narrow passage.

Things of no importance filled her mind. It was not,
as she had supposed, black or grey forbidding rock.
There were trees here, stunted and struggling it was true,
but they clad the mountain walls with greenery and brief
splashes of colour. They were too low, and she knew
that they would never be able to climb the steep walls
at the end of the canyon. It was the end of her search,
and a fatalistic numbness invaded her limbs as she stared
ahead.

They soared up though, the pilot praying fervently in
his own language as the small and battered plane reached
to the clear blue sky. They almost made it. They were
so close to the rock face at the very top that she could
see the shadow of the plane as closely as one sees a

shadow on the pavement when walking down a sunny
street, and they cleared the top, skimming the trees on
the further side, a side that was thickly forested with tall
pine trees.

It seemed, though, that the heart had gone from the
small plane. The engine stalled and spluttered, kicked
into life again to renew hope uselessly, and then died.

There was the sound of the wind to remind her of the
speed of their descent, the growing reality of tall trees
and then the sound of buckling metal, crashing branches
and nothing more as some great blow seemed to be aimed
at her head and the sunny day became empty, lifeless
and dark.

It might have been the tearing noise of the explosion
that brought her round from the depths of unconsciousness; she did not know. Whatever it was, she awoke
in time to see the enormous flash that followed the blast,
and to see the debris flying across the clearing—metal,
charred leather and innumerable small things flung into
the air, to be lost for ever.

Only the fact that she was sheltered by an outcrop of
rock saved her from further injury as, for frightening
seconds, the air was filled with danger. Then, as suddenly as it had begun, it was over. There was the crackle
of fire, drifting smoke, and she raised her head carefully
to look over the rocks that had saved her life.

Pain, fierce and savage, blinding and nauseating,
washed over her, making her moan, her hands coming
to her head as the pain momentarily blacked out her
sight. There was blood on her fingers when she looked
at them, blood from her head, and she knew she had
been injured in the crash, although she had no memory
of it.

The plane was hanging in the trees, suspended about several feet above the ground, and flames rose from it to engulf the treetops with brilliant red and yellow tongues of destruction, the heat from it suddenly focusing her attention as a wild kind of panic shot through her. There was no sign of the pilot. She could see around the clearing. Fate had given her the only tall outcrop of rocks. Either he was dead and in the burning plane, or he had staggered clear and was somewhere in the forest. Whatever his fate had been, she was now alone, and the need to get away from those searing flames drove her to her feet. There was no one here to help her.

She grasped the rocks, noticing with an almost detached interest that there was blood on her arm too, as well as mud and grass stains. Her skirt was torn and one shoe was missing altogether, but it did not matter. To get to her feet was an effort that seemed at first to be beyond her capabilities. The whole forest seemed to sway and turn, adding to her feeling of nausea, but she knew she must move as far and as fast as she could. It was unlikely that anyone would find her here, but it would be better to die beneath the cool pine trees than to die in the spreading blaze from the plane.

She had moved a long way when she finally fell for the last time and rolled down a steep slope, coming to a stop by the trunk of a mighty tree, a tree that seemed to have been there since time began. Turning her aching head, she could see a mountain, soaring and imperious, a long way off, visible owing to its sheer size. It looked across the land and seemed to frown on her, its mighty head capped with snow. A faint rise of smoke came from the summit and slowly, dreamily, she realised that it was a volcano.

It seemed to have an awareness, its attention directed at her alone, and the thought came to her mind that she would never leave this land, that she would die here beneath the trees, the great god of the mountain watching mercilessly. Blackness entered her mind, wiping out pain and distress, terror and loneliness, as her head became still and she lay in the forest like a pale and slender sacrifice to the white-haired god of the mountain.

He stood at the crest of the hill, his eyes scanning the precipitous slope. There was no expression on the handsome, dark face, no flicker of feeling in the black and intelligent eyes. She was here and he would find her. There had been no sign of her near to the burned-out wreckage of the plane, her body not close to the pilot's. She must have been flung clear, because there had been no evidence whatever that she had died in the fire when the plane had exploded and burned.

He glanced at his watch. Four hours! Not long when the terrain was so difficult and rocky, but long enough when injuries were severe. She had been capable of movement, and that was the hope. The rescue party was split into groups, searching the higher slopes, expecting to find her dead, but he had chosen to descend, some certainty in his mind that she would move downhill, though the going was hard even for anyone well equipped for the task. She would have suffered on these slopes— if she had survived at all. He thrust the thought from his mind and moved further out into the heat of the afternoon sunlight.

It was the volcano that brought her to his attention. She was lying at the foot of a tree at the very bottom of the steep gradient that opened into the sharply inclined clearing, and the tree seemed to be a finger of warning pointing to the sky and to the soaring grandeur of the white-capped mountain. So far, the sun had not touched her, for she was still in the shadow of the branches, only the bright colour of her hair making her clearly visible. A slight frisson of alarm raced through him, a feeling that he had not experienced since childhood.

'When the gods have chosen, let no man intrude!'

The words rang in his mind. He had heard it often in the villages of the Indians and smiled at it, ignored it, but now it had a sinister ring, no longer amusing.

He thrust such thoughts away and moved down towards her, his movements economical and swift, his dark eyes on her glowing hair. She was breathing, very shallow breaths it was true, but she was alive. The bright hair, coloured like the leaves of autumn, was tangled and streaked with blood, the colour somehow shocking against the tawny blaze of her hair. He knelt quickly to feel her pulse, his fingers on the slender column of her neck, his hand lingering to satisfy himself that the slight pulse was indeed there.

She had taken a blow to the temple and she was a mass of minor cuts and bruises, but otherwise she seemed to be all right. It was miraculous that this slip of a girl could walk away from a crash like that.

He stood, unclipping the two-way radio from his belt and raising the aerial.

'I have found her! Move south in a direct line with the plane. Hurry with that stretcher.'

'She is alive, Jaime?' The radio crackled into life as the question was asked, and he frowned, his dark face darkening even further.

'Yes. She needs treatment, though. Hurry, *por Dios*!'

He slammed the aerial back into place, fastening the radio back out of his way, his eyes drawn again to the white-capped volcano, in spite of his ready dismissal of it before, and he did not see the deep blue eyes open.

He seemed to be towering over her like a god, a god in a khaki bush shirt with shoulder tabs, with matching trousers that fitted tightly across his lean hips, high boots that protected his strong legs, and all that Sara could see of the man was the darkness of his skin, the utter midnight-black of his hair, and she sighed. Help had come, after all.

'I'm hurt.' It was not a complaint but a whispered statement, the voice little more than a breath, shadowy and low. 'I never thought that anyone would come.'

At the sound of her voice he spun round to look down at her, and then dropped to one knee, his dark eyes piercingly intent on her pale face as her eyes closed again. His voice too was low, but commanding.

'Sara!' He said her name with all the sound of authority, ordering her back to consciousness, and the effect was electric. The deep blue eyes shot open as she pulled herself from the soothing darkness that eased the pain.

'You!' She tried to move, to sit up, but his hand was hard and impelling on her arm, forbidding such movement. '*No!* Oh, no!' Further colour drained from her face until she was chalky-white, and as he made a swift movement towards her she slid back into unconsciousness, escaping from him in the best way possible, the only way.

CHAPTER THREE

SARA spent her time in a state of unreality. The shock of the accident had left her slightly disoriented, and concussion added to the feeling. She was somewhat battered and bruised, and at first had needed pain-killing drugs, but she was strong and determined, pulling herself back to health as quickly as possible, still marvelling that she had escaped so lightly from the crash.

She still did not remember the impact, but the rest was clear. At first when she had come round, she had imagined that her glimpse of Jaime Carreras had been a moment's nightmare brought on by shock, but she was now no longer in the stiff white hospital gown, she was in a beautiful satin nightdress, one of several that she seemed to have acquired, and she had a dreadful conviction that her benefactor was the tall, arrogant Mexican, and that one day soon she would be expected to account for her misdoings.

Her questions about this and any other thing brought only smiles and regretful shrugs. Nobody spoke English, it seemed, and this only added to the feeling that she was under threat. She had no doubts about the source of that particular feeling. The name Carreras had become mixed up in her mind with the country, with Mexico, the place she had known of for most of her life and had hated for years with a fierce hatred that, deep inside, she knew was illogical.

The fact that her father had chosen to desert his wife and child for this land was not in any way the fault of

the land itself, it was a fault of her father, but the anger
and pain that the name brought to her was far beyond
the bounds of logic, and the outrageous behaviour of
Jaime Carreras had only added to it. Now she was in
his land, and for the moment she was helpless.

The sound of the door opening made her look round
sharply, the quick movement adding to the pain already
in her head. She expected to see only the doctor, but
this time her dread was fully realised and she stifled her
quick burst of fear as her gaze fell on the tall, dark figure
of the man who strode uninvited into the room.

Of course, she had known that he would come. After
all, she had disobeyed him. Now was the day of
reckoning!

'Ah! You are fully awake this time!' There was a rather
cruel satisfaction in his voice that made her tighten up
inside even further, and he looked at her with unreadable dark eyes.

'You may speak. I know that you are almost recovered, miraculous though that seems to me. I have
kept an eye on your progress from a discreet distance,
knowing that you were safely trapped. There is nobody
here who understands English, therefore there is no one
to help you with busy plans.'

The information was sardonic, and there was a tone
of cold amusement in his voice as he walked slowly to
the bed and spoke again.

'Why are you surprised to see me? You did not imagine that I would leave you to your fate? You lost
everything in the fire when the plane burned. You would
have me abandon you to the care of strangers?'

The pallor of her face deepened, but the blue eyes that
met his were defiant.

'What do you mean, abandon me?' She fought down the rather desperate feeling of being in a net, and met his gaze with her head high, painful though it was. 'I'm nothing to you! I would certainly rather be left to strangers than be at your mercy!'

He seemed to find her words amusing, although his eyes were certainly not smiling.

'I have very little mercy as far as you are concerned, *señorita*,' he informed her coolly. 'I warned you of the dangers of a lone trip to this country. I also told you that you would find that all roads lead to Carreras. You now see that they do. When you are able to leave the hospital, you will come to me.' His gaze was almost hypnotic, and fear flared up inside her.

'*No!* I don't want to!' She was trying to fight this, her mind in a turmoil as she saw the hard satisfaction on his face, but he merely smiled, a cold gesture that went no further than his lips.

'Of course you do! That is why I am here. You are not as badly injured as we feared, but you are still shocked. For the next few days you must stay here and be cared for. When you are better, I will collect you!'

'I have no intention of coming to you or being anywhere near you!' she snapped, her head aching with the effort. It was hard to concentrate, to be firm, but she was fairly certain that if she did not fight her way out of this now she would never be able to.

'Really?' The black eyes flashed with sardonic amusement. 'Where else would you go? You have chosen to bring yourself to my country, to place yourself in a position where you are in desperate need of help. Who else is there to help you? After all, we are not strangers.'

'I wish to God that we were!' she blazed, and the effort almost had her dizzy. Her blue eyes flared at him, and for the first time he smiled, his dark, handsome face wryly amused, a quizzical sparkle in their black depths.

'You must rest. Believe me, you are safe. When you are better I will attend to all your problems. Perhaps I will even allow you to return to England.'

She looked at him quietly, her eyes narrowed with pain and frustration, her face now faintly flushed. For a second, her lips trembled, and she took a small breath that clearly hurt her. 'I intend...'

'Your intentions are very clear to me, *señorita*,' he said softly. 'Perhaps I should also make my intentions clear to you. You have been a nuisance and a disturbing influence from the moment that I met you. You have discarded advice which was carefully given. You have made it quite plain that your only aim in life is to chase wealth, and you have done that wilfully and dangerously!' He took a threatening step closer. '*I* rescued you, *señorita*!' he reminded her. 'I knew that you were coming and I knew where you would land! Had I not known, you would now be lying in the forest below the mountains, and you would probably be dead, for few people go there!' The black eyes narrowed to points of fire. 'You were wily enough to follow your selfish path regardless of others, in spite of my intervention, *señorita*,' he finished quietly. 'Then, of course, I was in your country. Now, you are in *mine*!'

'You—you wouldn't dare!' She stared at him, trapped by the black, glittering gaze, a panic-stricken huskiness in her voice.

'I do not recall having threatened anything at all, *señorita*,' he said with a cruelly amused look, 'but if your mind is dwelling on the past, then I did offer you an alternative source of wealth. You are now conveniently close, and of course, the offer is still open. You

could look around, consider other offers, but I very
much doubt if you will find anyone with a fortune to
match mine!'

She stiffened in anger, and only the realisation that
he did not mean it, but was merely trying to make her
feel shame, kept fright from her eyes.

'You're disgusting!'

'I have been called many things, *señorita*,' he said with
raised brows, 'but never disgusting. I do not recall feeling
disgust in you when I kissed you.'

She blushed furiously, suddenly unable to meet his
eyes. It was hurting her to battle, and he seemed to realise it, because he withdrew some of the intensity that
had been about him.

'Go to sleep!' he ordered with a softening of his tone.
'I will see you tomorrow. Perhaps soon they will release
you into my care. It cannot be too comfortable for you
here in this small and barren hospital. We are still too
close to the mountains for any luxurious medical care,
but they know what they are about or I would not have
left you here. Still, it will be nice to have someone with
you who can speak your own language, yes?'

'Providing that it's not you!' she managed, although
she felt dizzy now and quite sick.

He did not take the bait. Instead he suddenly laughed
and walked to the door, his hand raised in a brief and
indifferent farewell.

Several days later Sara was ready to leave, her immediate future in the strong and powerful hands of a man
she had hoped never to see again, a man who had found
her on a mountainside and taken charge of her life. She
needed to get away from him fast, because there was a
look of cold determination about him, and he was not

the sort of man to swallow his pride when he had been disregarded.

Carreras had brought her everything that she needed, carefully monitoring her progress so that he knew exactly when she was ready to leave, yet it had not been with any kindness. It had been with an attitude of duty and a certain detachment that had left her feeling afraid after his brief visits.

She sat on the edge of her bed, dressed and waiting, her heart taking on the usual hammering pace as he walked into the room.

'Ah! You are dressed and all ready to go?'

Sara's face grew hot at the smokily smooth voice. Yes, she was dressed to leave, dressed in clothes that she could never have afforded herself. Every item of clothing that she possessed, every small luxury, had been provided by the tall Mexican who now regarded her with no expression whatever in his eyes.

His face was burnished by the sun, hawklike and strong, the brilliant black of his eyes a compelling force that stemmed any kind of dissent. His black hair was thick, shining and utterly without wave. He was handsome, powerful and arrogant, and he frightened her, made her angry and wary. Common sense told her that he was a civilised man, a well-educated and well-known man, not able to follow his inclinations and insist that she stay with him and keep out of trouble, but she still remembered his fury, the hurtful words he had used. She still remembered his cold expectation of her compliance with his demands.

Sara realised that she was staring up at him, probably like a rabbit watching a stoat or, in this particular case, like a deer watching a mountain lion.

'When you are quite ready!' he said caustically, clearly reading her expression and liking it not one bit. 'Or do you have worries—*extra* worries?'

'This is a very beautiful dress,' she said rather sharply, looking down at the flowing skirt of the dress in question, the sharp colours of the exquisite pattern holding her eyes. 'The shoes too are—are lovely.'

'You do not seem to be too happy about it.' His dark voice was not amused. 'You would have preferred to leave the hospital still dressed as you have been while in your bed? It can be arranged.'

'I didn't mean that at all! It—it's just that—that you seem to have been buying me a lot of things, and I don't know how I'll ever be able to repay you.'

'Should you even think of it, I would be most annoyed!'

He walked towards her and stood looking down into her face, a very beautiful face, even though she had lost weight during her stay in the hospital.

'Everything that you possessed in this country was lost in the fire. What would you have had me do?' He suddenly reached for her arm, his face rather irritated. 'Come, let us go! I trust that you are not about to be consumed with guilt every time I decide to buy something for you? You are in my care! Please take note of that word, because I intend to care for you. Naturally you will need to be clothed and fed.' He shot her a flashing, dark-eyed glance. 'Think of yourself as a little stray who is to be pampered—you will then get the picture.'

She glared at him, but he wasn't even looking. That firm, sensuous mouth, those shuttered eyed told her that she was a nuisance, but that his mind was made up.

'You won't need to care for me!' she said sharply. 'All I need is the use of a telephone and someone who speaks English. I came here to get to my father, and I intend to do just that. My own Embassy will help me!'

The dark eyebrows raised sardonically as he watched her flushed and angry face with some amusement.

'You have great faith in your flag, *señorita*,' he murmured quietly. 'What should I say to you that will not dampen your spirits, except perhaps, "We will see"?'

He suddenly tired of amusement and took her arm firmly, lifting up her new suitcase—another thing he had provided—and leading her out into the sunshine.

It was astonishingly hot outside once the cool shade of the hospital was left behind, and she was glad to get into the dark, air-conditioned car that waited for them.

Seated, and facing forward, she could see the towering height of a volcano, the mere size of it awesome, compellingly beautiful as it stood in mighty splendour against a backdrop of brilliantly blue sky. There was something fateful about it that frightened her, and her mind recognised her helplessness, the giant mountain sharpening her realisation that she was in an alien land, a cold stranger beside her.,

There was no sign of warmth in him, no comforting glimmer of gentleness or pity. The look on his face was one of dislike and, after all, it was only what she could have expected. Why was she going with him to a house she did not know? Surely it would be better to escape while she was here? But she had no passport, no papers, no money. There was no help here, nobody who spoke her language. She had tried that. She would have to change her plans, because deep inside she knew now that nobody but Jaime Carreras would help her to find her father, and he had said no in cold, insulting terms.

'Something is troubling you, *señorita*?'

Carreras was watching her, the engine quietly idling, his powerful arm across the wheel as he sat sideways his eyes on her face. She looked into those eyes, not answering. They were like a midnight sky: bottomless, hypnotic, pitiless, the thick, glossy, black lashes curled against his skin, outlining the liquid darkness of his gaze. It was difficult to admit for somebody of her spirit, but he frightened her.

'I was wondering about your house, that's all,' she said quickly, feeling that she must hide her thoughts from him, thoughts that were now a turmoil inside her head because she had made up her mind that she would get him to take her to her father whether he liked it or not!

He watched her for a minute with unreadable eyes.

'It is several miles away. My home is in the foothills. I believe that we have the best of both worlds there. You remember the mountain where I found you? It is hot under the sun but cold at night. Here in Mexico the climate is very variable, depending upon where you are. There are pine forests on the higher slopes of the mountains, snow that is permanent on the highest peaks, but come down to sea level and you have a tropical climate, like another world. My house is old, dating from the days of the Spanish rule, and it has been in my family for generations. The sooner that we get started, the sooner you will see it, and then you will understand exactly what I mean.'

'Do you live there alone?' she asked in a hurried, breathless little voice. His black eyes narrowed to focus sharply on her, making her want to duck her head in case he read her mind.

'You fear for your life?' he asked scathingly. 'You will be quite safe. There are servants enough to fall over should you not watch your step, but more than that, there are two other ladies there who are under my protection.' He threw his head back and smiled wryly at her expression. 'Ah, no, I do not make a habit of collecting distressed females as others collect stamps! The two ladies are members of my family, in a manner of speaking. There is my stepmother and her daughter. They live with me permanently. So you see, there is really nothing to fear from me.'

'I don't . . . I never for one moment imagined that . . .'

'Oh, I did not think for one moment either that you feared rape and molestation. I do think, however, that the idea of murder has drifted into your mind, or perhaps slavery?' He was so derisive, so cold. 'Or perhaps the greater evil of being permanently restrained and unable to get to your father? Be at peace, *señorita*,' he urged with a sinister softness, 'I intend to take care of you and see that no harm whatever befalls you, only as long as is necessary. You told me that there was a time factor involved. We will wait out the time, then you may go. Meanwhile, I wish you to rest, be as happy as you can and get completely well.'

'I am well!' she said as firmly as she could. 'I know how I feel!'

'Perhaps I am speaking of the health of conscience!' he said tightly. 'We will not tread that particular path, *señorita*.'

She stared up at him in a fury; she just couldn't help it. It was going to be impossible to pretend to be sweet and pleasant, and try to win him round to helping her. He was abominable, even if he was handsome as the devil! He was more than handsome, she thought, her eyes widening as she looked at him, more than striking. He was brilliantly alive, and there was a power about him that was compelling. If he were there, no other man would be noticed. The thought, unexpected as it was, brought a bright blush to her face, and his eyes narrowed quickly.

'Let us go!' he said suddenly, turning from his harsh contemplation of her face, her rapt expression. Apparently just looking at her angered him, and she knew that it would be difficult to get round this man, especially as she hated him! She turned away herself, tightly angry both with him and with her wayward mind.

Carreras was the only one who could help her, and she knew that, but how could she get him to do it? He would blame her for every thought in her head, every word that came out of her mouth. Perhaps he even thought she had crashed on purpose? A wild little feeling of amusement shot through her, a light, hysterical feeling, and she turned away to hide her eyes, a sound of protest low in her throat at this unseemly need to laugh.

He mistook it for fear.

'Save your terror, *señorita*!' he snapped, getting the car on the move. 'You have some time during which I shall consider you to be an invalid, a few days at least. It will give your agile mind some time in which to think of a plan!'

'I already have a plan, Señor Carreras!' she said bitingly. 'I need not explain it to you. You already know. I intend to find my father!'

'You may find that *my* plans interfere with this scenario!' he rasped. 'Your wings, *señorita*, are well and truly clipped. You are a bird in my hand, a captured magpie whom heaven disguises as a dove. The disguise, though, is not now important. It is the word "captured" that should dwell in your mind!'

He accelerated with a force that was alarming, and she heard the deep breath in his voice, her brain trying to work out just how isolated they were, just how powerful he was, and whether the feelings inside her were fear or excitement.

The town where the hospital stood was built astride the main road, although it was stretching the imagination to call the road that, because it seemed to Sara to be merely a very wide track, dusty and potholed, with stones tossed up by passing vehicles lying like so many small traps along the whole length of it. It wound up into the hills, and in the distance she could see the hazy blue of a mountain range, rather alarming even from here.

'You can now see the mountains that rise behind my home,' Jaime said after a while, apparently having partly recovered from his attack of displeasure. 'They are in fact some distance away, but the view from the house is quite spectacular. You will be able to see them from your bedroom.'

'I've never seen mountains like that before,' Sara ventured quietly, trying to be very good, and earning herself a sharp glance.

'Certainly not in your own country,' he assured her. 'Mexico is a mountainous country, but in actual fact, we have everything—tropical beaches, lushly green lowlands and indeed, plenty of land. Unfortunately, much of it is straight upwards!'

'Don't you like the mountains?'

She found herself watching him, noticing not for the first time the high forehead and the proudly jutting nose. There seemed to be nothing about him that would lead one to believe that he had any lenient tendencies in him, and once again she wondered why he had taken on the responsibility for her welfare simply to keep her from a man he did not now know.

He was an influential man; certainly, he had made waves in London, and there had been a great flurry in the hospital every time he'd been due to arrive. He was rich and important, well known in other countries besides his own, and it would have been an easy matter for him to have her put on a plane for England, to stop her from getting any permission to return. Could it mean that he intended some sort of revenge for her attitude to his advice? The idea was preposterous, but it came to her anyway.

'I love the mountains,' he answered quietly after a glance at her. 'There is peace there that is not found elsewhere. However, I rarely get the chance to simply roam at will in the mountains. If I am not in the city on business, then I am working among the Indians, often for months at a time.'

'Just reappearing when you want to!' she said a trifle starchily, irritated by his ability to do exactly as he liked, which included interfering in her affairs.

'There are those who would like it well if I never reappeared,' he said drily. 'If I had not been there when your small plane crashed though, *señorita*, you might never have been found, or you might have been left exactly as you lay, a beautiful tribute to the gods!'

'I've no doubt that the barbaric past is still very much to the fore here!' Sara said tartly, relaxing her attitude of amiability for a second. 'I cannot simply disappear, though. I'm a British citizen!'

'Proudly said!' he rasped sardonically. 'It is a long way to the glitter of the British Embassy when you are in the mountains here. Try to remember that!'

His words silenced her. Her hands clenched in her lap, and she turned her head away stiffly.

They were close to the mountains now, and she could see that they were not barren. Trees covered the lower slopes, and they climbed up until their heads were lost in the clouds. Beside the road too, flowers grew, brightly coloured and delicate, some she felt she should recognise, their purples and pinks interspersed with brilliant yellow. They were growing wild, adding a soft beauty to the dusty roadside, taking away the stark fact that this was a neglected and lonely part of the world.

'The road is very rough,' she commented after a while, when it became apparent that he was not about to speak and the silence had become too much for her.

'Oh, we are forcing the main highway through, and soon, one day, it will reach here,' he said quietly. 'When it comes, the necessary evil of tourists will follow, I expect. One has to decide upon one's priorities. I accept the constant damage to my cars when the alternative is the type of progress that I can do without. I prefer solitude!'

'Like being in the Indian villages?' she intervened quietly, hearing a kind of sadness in his voice that she had never suspected could be there.

'*Claro!* It is my life. It is the way I have chosen to live my life!' He spoke sharply, clearly not wanting to discuss his affairs with her, and certainly not wanting any softness. Sara knew that it would be better to keep quiet, and she turned back to her contemplation of the road as he also remained silent.

There were small villages along their route, tidy and colourful places, and now the flowers were brilliant, a kaleidoscope of colour and luxury after the wild flowers left that grew beside the road. The walls of the houses were white, with purple blossom spilling to the ground and climbing to the roofs, and the walled gardens gave sudden and secret glimpses of rose bushes, vivid tulips, marigolds and fruits.

But mountains now took all her attention—not just the majesty of them as they towered over the landscape, making her feel small and insignificant, but the relentless constancy. Mountain behind mountain, each one higher than the other; they seemed to be endless, a barrier that was impassable. The road now wound its way upwards and a new anxiety entered her mind, taking away some of the awe of the view. They were travelling along a road that clung to the mountain wall, a sheer drop of hundreds of feet beside them, the road little more than a rough track, and her muscles tightened involuntarily.

'You are afraid?' He glanced quickly at her, and then fixed his eyes firmly on the road.

'I'll let you know!' said Sara in a tight voice, and suddenly he gave a quiet laugh, a mere chuckle of sound that was comfort and encouragement.

'It is a little nerve-racking, perhaps, for someone not accustomed to the mountains,' he agreed. 'When you have spent your whole life among them, you tend not to notice too much that there are chasms beside the road. You can close your eyes, of course.'

'No, thank you!' She took a deep breath and stopped trying to guess whether or not it was a mile down to the winding track of a dry riverbed that she could see below. 'With my eyes closed, I'll not know when we're going over!'

'I assure you that we are not going over,' he said. 'It is daylight and I am quite sober. There is nothing to fear except fear itself.' He looked at her with a sidelong glance of flashing dark eyes, and she nodded pertly to the road.

'Thank you for the invigorating speech. Please keep looking straight ahead.'

He obeyed her at once, but his lips were still curved in a smile when he said quietly, 'I am not punishing you. I would have spared you this if it had been possible, but there is no other way to approach the house. Very soon we shall see it.'

'Do you drive along here at night?' she asked in an awe-stricken voice, quite forgetting to be angry. It was alarming how she was beginning to feel a growing security from his presence.

'I have done, but it is not a good idea to drive at all at night in this part of the country. There are often unexpected obstacles. Even on the main road. A car breaks down and is abandoned, there are no lights, and you can be upon it before you realise the fact. Animals too have the habit of wandering about in the road at night. We tend to count the sundown as a time when the day is over as far as travelling is concerned. Even if we are flying in, we try to time our arrival for the hours of daylight.'

'You have a plane?' Why this should have astonished her she did not know. If he lived here, so far away from civilisation, then he would have to be able to get out of here fast whenever he needed to. Maybe he would fly her out of here?

'Sí, my plane is kept at the small airfield just outside the town. I have a private secretary who lives with us at the house, and he also doubles as a pilot for me. I rarely fly myself. Normally I am too busy catching up on paperwork when I am travelling.

'Your secretary is a man?' Sara was secretly glad of that. For some reason she was very anxious about meeting the two women at the Carreras house, and the fact that there was another person living there too was a relief, especially as it was a man. She wasn't at all sure why the thought gave her comfort, but it did, nevertheless. Perhaps it was because there had been little happiness in her life, except for William.

'Most definitely! You will probably like him, as he is unlike me!' he snapped, relenting a little as he added, 'Certainly he will like you. Hernando is usually taken with the ladies. I will have to see that he has too much work to bother you unduly.'

'Am I to be isolated from all male companionship?' she asked a trifle daringly, but he was not even slightly amused.

'The thought had occurred to me, in view of your commitment to this William, but we will have to see how you cope with life at the house. I expect that you will survive even without any protection from me. Perhaps you will survive better than I do. Women have the intrinsic ability to shake the ground beneath a man's feet.'

'There won't be time for me to shake any ground!' Sara said tightly, forgetting her new plan. 'I shall be going!'

'When I let you!' he said softly, back to quiet mockery. 'Meanwhile, there is the house.'

He was not about to say any more and, after a worried glance at him, she looked across the yawning chasm to see for the first time the house where she was to make her home for the next week, or even longer. Her future was in the determined hands of this man, and she could not at the moment break free. She didn't want to even think about the frightening implications, but for as long as she was here, in Mexico, there was a chance to get to her father. Whatever she had to do, she was sure that she could do it.

The house nestled close to the foothills of the mountains, and there was a stately beauty about it that held her attention. From so far off it was possible to take a good look at it from an unusual angle, because it was quite clear that they would once again have to descend to reach the house. From this eagle-eye view she could see the gardens surrounding it, the buildings that were probably servants' quarters, the great outer wall that surrounded the whole property, and the tree-filled gardens, bright with colour even from here.

'There's a pool!' The glitter of water had caught her eye, and she could not stop the excited exclamation.

'Certainly. It can be very hot here, and a swimming pool is more of a necessity than a luxury. I hope that you will enjoy using the pool. Do you swim?' His sensuous lips quirked. 'But why should I ask? It is a thing that is easily discovered. We will simply throw you in. María-Teresa will like that, no doubt.'

'María-Teresa?' She looked at him anxiously, and received a quick, sardonic glance.

'My stepmother's daughter,' he informed her shortly. 'Or to be less obscure, my stepsister. I cannot think that she will take to you very easily. She is eighteen, and well aware of her own female powers already.'

'I'm not at all sure what you mean,' she said quickly, her heart suddenly racing with anxiety.

'I mean that she will probably not appreciate the fact that you are to stay in my house for any length of time, or even for any time at all.'

'But why? I haven't even met her yet! How could I possibly offend her?'

Carreras shot her a look of pure irony, his laughter soft and sardonic. 'Neither my stepmother nor my stepsister welcome beautiful *señoritas* into the house,' he assured her. 'They like to rule the domain like queens in double harness. Only their—indulgence towards me has stopped a crisis at the thought of your arrival.'

Indulgence! He meant fear! And now she felt plenty of it herself.

'Why are you doing this to me?' she asked heatedly, her eyes on his hard profile.

'But I have rescued you, *señorita*!' he said with mocking astonishment. 'I have cared for you, clothed you, and now I intend to keep an eye on you for a short while!'

'I won't change my mind about what I intend to do!' she said coldly, more alarmed than she would ever admit to this arrogant man.

'We will see, *señorita*!' he replied with an equal coldness that seemed to cloud the hot sunshine as he drew slowly to the high gates in the wall that surrounded the house and grounds.

The gates were heavy, oaken gates studded with brass, old Spanish gates that were opened at his blast on the horn by two white-clad servants, their sombreros tipped over their dark faces. Sara glanced at them as they drove past, her muscles tensing. They were colourful, calm-looking, but to her they suddenly took on the look of gaolers. What would they do if she walked down here and demanded in an imperious voice that they open the gate?

Señor Carreras, apparently, could read minds.

'A warning, *señorita*!' he said sharply. 'The grounds are patrolled at nights by a very ferocious dog. He is so effective, in fact, that keeping more than one dog has proved to be unnecessary. Walk where you will during the day; he is then confined. At night, however, call to me if you feel compelled to move further than the patio. You are a stranger, and he does not take to strangers!'

'I shall not forget, Señor Carreras!' she said as smoothly as she could. Here, then, was the threat. During the day there would no doubt be plenty of the white-clad servants to watch her. At night, she would be a prisoner.

They drove through beautiful gardens bright with towering poinsettias and magnolia bushes and, although determination still ruled her mind, Sara knew a miserable feeling of inevitability as he drew up by the massive front doors.

'Welcome to my home, Señorita Lawrence,' he said softly. 'My house is your house.'

An old Mexican custom, no doubt, but to Sara he might equally have said, 'My house is your prison.' It felt like that!

CHAPTER FOUR

THE HALL was spacious and cool, furnished not as she had somehow expected, with heavy furniture to match the rather brooding Spanish architecture of the house, but with light modern tables of beautiful design. There were bowls of flowers everywhere, and the parquet floor shone like glass. Jaime Carreras did not linger here however, but, taking her arm again, he headed for one of the rooms at the side of the hall and opened the door.

He was throwing her into this without any form of consultation, and Sara had no idea what to expect. She suddenly had the frantic desire to cling to his arm, to hang on to the only person she knew, even though that person was Jaime Carreras, but no time for thought or action was given.

The room was obviously the *sala*, and the thing that Sara noticed most was the wide expanse of carpet—a lovely blue, deep and luxurious. It set the colour scheme for the whole room. There were settees in delicately patterned covers, lamps on dark polished tables, deep easy-chairs in white and, everywhere, flowers and plants. It was a beautiful room, with huge windows opening on to the garden, the long curtains drawn back to let in the sun, and standing facing them both were the two women she had dreaded meeting.

'My stepmother, Constanza,' he introduced courteously, 'and her daughter, María-Teresa Lopez de Ferrer.' He urged Sara forward politely, presenting her with an air of one who will suffer no interference.

'Señorita Sara Lawrence,' he said coldly, adding, 'As you know, she is to stay here as my guest!'

Sara was still digesting the surprise of the length of name of María-Teresa when the girl broke into a deluge of rapid Spanish, but he put a stop to that at once.

'You will please address me in English while Sara is here,' he said, with a smile at the girl which took any sting out of the words.

It was all that Sara could do to stop gaping at him. He had called her Sara! His manner was friendly! A deep suspicion formed in her mind that he had told these two a story that was very wide of the truth! Her eyes flashed to his face, and to her astonishment he was smiling down at her pleasantly. For the life of her, she could not return that smile.

'Will you sit down, Señorita Lawrence?' Constanza Carreras motioned gracefully to one of the high-backed white chairs, remembering her position here and attempting to put on some face in view of Jaime's dominance. She was a woman in her late fifties, still attractive, but with a fretful, dissatisfied look about her mouth that robbed her of any real beauty. Sara moved forward uneasily, but before she could sit down Jaime took her arm, stationing her firmly beside him in front of the old fireplace that was now filled with flowers.

'I think that perhaps Sara would like to settle in her room first,' he said quietly, his hand warningly on Sara's arm. 'The journey from the hospital has tired her a little. She will come down to join us when she has freshened up and settled her things.'

'I—er—thank you, I do feel a little dazed!' Sara said with just enough sarcasm to have the hand tightening from warning to threat.

'It was a miracle that you survived the accident, Señorita Lawrence,' María-Teresa put in quickly. 'If Jaime had not been expecting you, I think that you would still have been in the mountains. He was able to organise a very rapid search. Naturally, the crash was reported to him first.'

Naturally! Sara tried to look grateful and demure, but her mind was seething with questions. Jaime Carreras would have some explaining to do the moment that they were alone. For the moment she was prepared to hold her tongue and go along with anything he said.

If she told these two women that he had been ordering her, a complete stranger, to follow his rules while she was still in her own country, and that he had virtually forced her to be here, then he would perhaps feel obliged to return her to England. She did not want that at all. There was no money left for another flight to Mexico, and by then, in any case, the time would have run out.

He might also feel obliged to explain to the stiff and unfriendly Constanza, and the beautiful black-haired girl who stood with dark and watchful eyes, that Sara Lawrence was a self-seeking, greedy woman who was, in any case, no better than she should be! Sara didn't fancy that, either; already the air was thick with antagonism and enquiry.

'It was lucky that—Jaime found me so quickly,' Sara agreed, smiling sweetly at his stepsister. 'It was an unfortunate way to arrive in his country.'

'Never mind. You are here now, and everything is nicely settled,' he said with a look of approval at her use of his first name. Apparently her intelligence-rating had soared in his estimation, or more likely he thought that she was so used to intrigue and subterfuge that she had picked up his signal and reacted purely from instinct.

The two women were watching her so closely that Sara now wanted to get up to her room with great speed and have a quiet chat with her captor before she faced them again. It was a relief when he rang the bell and a servant appeared at once.

'This is Señorita Lawrence, Conchita,' he explained, looking into the dark face of the old woman, who stood waiting with no sign of alarm. 'You now have the opportunity to practise all the English that I have taught you over the years. While she is here, you will speak to her in her own language, and address me only in English in her presence.'

She nodded with a bright-eyed smile at Sara, her old face breaking into a wide grin, showing two or three gold teeth as Jaime added, 'When I am not available, she is in your care.'

'I am honoured, Señor Jaime,' she said, with little surprise at this statement.

She was obviously comfortable with him, and there was certainly a lessening of the autocratic power in him when he addressed her.

'I will take care of her. She is beautiful,' Conchita remarked with a knowing look.

Her grin widened when he urged her out with the words, 'Your eyes are sharp, Conchita, but watch the ease of your tongue. Call someone to get the *señorita*'s suitcase, and then take Señorita Lawrence to her room.'

'Really, Jaime!' Constanza Carreras exploded quietly when the woman had gone. 'Must you treat that old woman like a confidante? Already she has far too much liberty here! Naturally, when you are not available, María-Teresa and I will see that the *señorita* is taken care of!'

'I am sure that you would,' he purred smoothly. 'However, Conchita is here to do the job for you, and she is answerable only to me. Do not forget that I have known her all my life. She was my nurse when I was a child, and even now she scolds me when she thinks that I have strayed from the narrow path. Who better to guard Sara?'

To *guard* her? The very use of the word made Sara's blood run cold. He had meant every word he had said, then! What exactly had he told these two?

'I would not wish my physical state to be discussed with that old Indian woman!' María-Teresa remarked sulkily, her eyes on Sara's hair and face. 'Do you not object, Señorita Lawrence?'

'I'm certain that Jaime knows best, for the moment,' Sara answered quickly. 'I'm still a little shaky after the accident. I'll be quite capable of taking care of myself after a few days. In any case, I'll be leaving soon.'

If there was some plan here, if Jaime had confided in them at all, then now was as good a time as any to find out.

'How touchingly dependent you are at the moment!' Constanza said quietly, with a wry look at Sara that had her cheeks flushing. 'How fortunate that you already know Jaime, otherwise you would be still in that dreadfully uncomfortable hospital, among strangers.'

'However, she is not!' Jaime said smoothly. 'In a few days she will be completely restored to health, and then we can all settle down peacefully.'

'How long will you be here, Señorita Lawrence?' María-Teresa began with a sharp glance at Sara, but Jaime stopped that line of questioning at once.

'We will tell you all about our plans at dinner time,' he said with an affectionate smile at her. 'You are always

too inquisitive, *querida*. Let Sara get her breath before
you pile questions on her. She is not as used to your
ways as I am. As to your remarks about Conchita's
Indian origins, we are all Mexicans! Do not alarm Sara
with any prejudices that you have. I want her to enjoy
her stay here. She will begin to imagine that we are
savages,' he added with a sly look at Sara that brought
angry color to María-Teresa's face, but which did not
fool Sara. He would never let a thing go by if it meant
that he could get a dig at her.

'I will see you later,' he said solicitously as Conchita
appeared at the door. 'You looked tired. Allow Conchita
to do everything for you. Perhaps you should have a
light lunch in your room and then rest? It is your first
day out of hospital, after all. You will be able to join
us for dinner tonight.'

Sara made a quick decision. It suited her well enough.
By tonight they would have their story worked out, or
at least he would be able to give her his latest orders
before then, and she wasn't about to fight it. She wanted
him to take her to her father, and she was beginning to
see that the two women here might just be the sort of
lever she needed. She smiled up at him winsomely.

'Thank you, Jaime,' she murmured sweetly. 'You're
very kind to me.' It almost caught him off guard!

She followed Conchita up the wide oak stairs. She was
a bit tired and very annoyed with her irritating captor.
He had had plenty of time on the way here to tell her
how he proposed to explain her captivity to his relatives.
From the look in María-Teresa's eyes, it was clear that
the girl did not feel like a relative anyway, and his attitude could only have antagonised her. Far from imagining that the Mexican girl would want to throw her
in the pool, he was deliberately engineering it! He had

actually managed to be very slightly seductive to two women at once down there! She wondered that he hadn't thrown Constanza in for good measure!

In fact, she was a bit frightened, but there was no way that he was going to discover that! Right now, she would have gladly been back in the little hospital, planning to get help from the Embassy. If Jaime had not known her, surely she would have been handed over to the authorities, and they would have arranged it. This was a civilised country, even though she hated it for her own reasons.

William must be worrying that she had not been in touch. She had been in Mexico for two weeks to her certain knowledge, maybe even longer than that. There had been a time when concussion had made her days a little hazy. Would Jaime forbid her to get in touch with William? In his present state of mind, she hardly dared to bring the subject up, but she would have to and very soon.

Power! Even when she had been in England, his name had spelled power. How much power did he have here? Could he force her to stay? In this day and age it was unlikely, but then, all this was unlikely! There were too many questions, and Jaime would have to answer them. She felt a burst of irritation as she realised that she was now thinking of him as Jaime, instead of as that arrogant Mexican. It would have to stop!

When Conchita left, she inspected the room. Like the *sala*, it had rich appointments—subtle shades of pink and blue on a background of cream. A woman's room. She recognised that, and she wondered who had had this room before her. Everything she was likely to need was on the dressing-table and, opening a door at the side of the room, she found an equally luxurious bathroom, the towels continuing the pink and blue theme. It was only what could be expected in the home of a very rich man. He was accustomed to doing and having exactly everything he wanted. He had added her to that list! He had decided to correct her outlook on life, or at least see to it that she did not have the chance to 'chase' this particular money.

She wandered around the room for a minute, touching things, gaining pleasure from the beauty, and then her eye fell on the wardrobe built into the wall at the other side of the room. She opened it and found, as she had dreaded, clothes there that were obviously for her and not just a few for a short stay. Had they belonged to anyone else, they would have been removed in this efficient household. Jaime would not tolerate inefficiency, she was sure of that. The colours were suitable for someone of her own colouring, and the sight of them was altogether too much, emphasising her feeling of being trapped and utterly alone, even though she planned to turn it to her advantage.

She left the door wide open and went to the long window, opening it and stepping out on to the balcony, staring at the mountains with unseeing eyes, thinking rapidly but reaching no conclusions.

She did not hear Jaime come into the room, her first intimation that he was there being when a hard hand grasped her arm as his voice rang harshly in her ears.

'Do not step out on to this balcony!' he ordered sternly, and before she could react at all she found herself drawn back into the room, the tall windows closed. Even the back of his neck looked angry. 'As yet, I do not know whether you will be subject to fainting spells,' he said, checking that the windows were indeed secure. 'It was mentioned at the hospital, and certainly you took a hard blow to the head and had concussion. Therefore, to go on the balcony is dangerous!' He turned towards her and his tone changed abruptly as he saw her face. 'Why are you looking like that?' he grated angrily. 'I am not locking you in your room! Taking unnecessary risks is out of the question. You are my guest. I am responsible for your welfare, and I am merely seeing that you do not harm yourself!'

Now was the time. She took a deep breath and faced him squarely.

'I want to telephone England!' she said as firmly as possible. 'I've been in hospital for two weeks and...'

'Three!' he corrected harshly. 'In fact you have been there for slightly longer than that. As I said, you have had concussion, badly. There were injuries and then there was the shock. It was, after all, an air crash!'

'Over three weeks!' It was longer than she had thought. William would be going mad with worry! 'I've *got* to telephone England! He—they—people will be anxious about me...'

'You came to seek your father, to trek into the mountains. Surely you had not anticipated that it would be possible to put in a call to England every night?' he enquired scathingly, his brow darkening. 'You are still with this man, then? I had wondered if, after my advice, you would be spreading your favours further afield!'

Sara's flat palm caught him across the face before she remembered the consequences of such an action, and his head snapped back with the force of it. She was wildly angry and completely forgot her plan. Her anger, though, could not compare with his.

'*Zorra!* That is twice!' He grasped her shoulders and hauled her against the power of his chest, his eyes blazing with fury. '*Dios!* Try that again and I will shake the breath from you, even if you have just survived an accident! Next time I might very well forget that you have injured your head, and shake it off!'

He was terrifying! It was very clear that nobody had ever had the temerity to stand up to him before, and that the slap she had given him in the park in London had been his first experience of physical reprisal. There was not one ounce of pity in his face, only the astonishment and fury that her slap had engendered. He, it seemed, could say anything he chose, hurl any kind of insults, while she was supposed to stand there and take it calmly. It infuriated her, and she forgot her fear in her own anger.

'Speak to me like that again and I'll do exactly the same or worse!' she blazed, struggling furiously to free herself from his iron grip. 'Let me go! I want to phone William and I'm *going* to phone William! Try to stop me and I'll get help from somewhere else!'

'From where?' He still held her fast, but his anger was now beginning to subside, no doubt because he was amused at her inability to get free or to carry out her wild threats. It made her struggle more, her hair falling over her face, her hands plucking uselessly at him until he gave her a quick shake.

'Stop this nonsense!' he said sharply. 'You are tiring yourself out. This will make you ill again!'

He was perfectly right, of course, and Sara stopped suddenly, realising that she was trembling uncontrollably. She felt quite shaken all at once, helpless. She had enough of a burden without this man tearing into her whenever he felt like it, without his interfering and domineering intrusion into her life.

'Let me go!' she said coldly, trying to keep the tremor from her voice. 'I admit to being temporarily trapped, but I will not submit to either insults or manhandling!'

'It is not, and never was my intention to manhandle you!' he said quietly. He sounded harassed, and she looked up into the brilliantly dark eyes, surprised to find his face neither angry nor sardonic. 'I have told you that you are irritating!' he said heavily, letting her go and turning away. 'I have a temper of my own, and you seem to bring it to the surface more quickly than any woman I have ever known. No doubt it is because you are English!' he added, turning to her with a gathering frown.

'No doubt!' Sara said bitingly. 'Perhaps Mexican women take readily to being ordered about. I do not!'

He looked frustratedly at her as she walked to the bed and sat on the edge of it.

'Does William "order you about"?' he asked unexpectedly. 'Do you fly into a rage and beat him when he tries to advise you?'

The unique idea brought a quirk to Sara's lips, and her eyes met the dark eyes that seemed to be watching her intently.

'I've known William for a long time, *señor*,' she said more quietly. 'We get along fine.'

'Obviously!' he snapped. 'You are staying with him, although he is not wealthy enough to take care of your desires apparently. He must have something else going for him!' He shrugged uninterestedly, dismissing William and her private life with the one gesture. 'You had better get used to calling me by my name, instead of this strictly formal way of speaking,' he added coolly when she simply sat there.

'I'm glad that you brought that up!' Sara said sharply. 'It's fortunate that I was able to field the fast one that you threw at me downstairs. You called me by my first name quite unexpectedly,' she explained irritably when his eyes merely widened at her expression. It gave her a small spurt of satisfaction that he was not completely knowledgeable about the English idiom.

'You were admirably quick,' he agreed with a slight smile. His raised eyebrows made her feel just slightly criminal, and her voice sharpened to match her annoyance.

'Perhaps, *señor*, it would be a good idea to tell me what *lies* you felt it necessary to use as an explanation of my presence here?'

His quick flare of anger was well worth the risk of calling him a liar, and he glowered at her briefly before explaining in a cold voice, 'I have told them that we knew each other in London. They know that you are here to look for your father, and for the time that will suffice! Should it be necessary to restrain you for any great length of time, I will think of something else!'

Sara ignored the cold attitude, the threat of further restraint. Her ears had heard exactly what they wished to hear.

'They'll expect you to take me to my father!' she said triumphantly, standing up in her eagerness. 'Are you going to take me, Jaime?'

Enthusiasm robbed her of any formality and he smiled slowly, walking forward to look down at her, his eyes glittering with amusement.

'At least you are never dull,' he said with laughter in his voice. 'And, yes, Sara, I do intend to take you to your father. Perhaps you should see him, after all. Maybe you will not then dislike him so much. However, do not get too excited. I will take you when the time is up and the money no longer in your grasp. Then, perhaps, you will be able to look at him and assess him without the glitter of gold blinding your eyes.'

'Then, *señor*, I will not have the faintest interest in going!' she snapped.

'You will go! It will be worth it just to see how you react to the hardships of the mountains,' he goaded. 'Perhaps by the time we get back to civilisation you will have forgotten all about William?'

'Never in a million years!' Sara replied, goading in her turn, her pert face sarcastic. If he was going to get annoyed, let him!

He did not get annoyed, however. Instead, he reached forward and captured her, laughing down into her eyes, and she became horrifyingly aware of an electric thrill of attraction and of the suddenly speculative look on his dark face.

'For a moment, in that cold park in England, you forgot all about William, *señorita*,' he said quietly. 'If I want you to forget him, you will!'

His smile of total superiority infuriated her out of any thrill, and she pulled against him, trying unsuccesfully to free herself, alarmed at the rising excitement that had started to surge through her.

'This is called kidnapping! Even in an uncivilised place like this, there must be some sort of law! You can't get away with it, and you know it!'

'I can get away with it for long enough,' he murmured, his eyes flaring over her breasts, tight against the bodice of her dress.

'You—you barbarian!' She shuddered at the look in his eyes, and his head snapped up, his dark gaze holding hers until her face flushed like a rose.

'You are talking yourself into trouble again, *señorita*!' he said softly, and this time she couldn't think of any reply, couldn't even move. She was back in England, back in the cold silence of the park, his hands stroking her face, his lips caressing. Wild excitement swept through her again, making her flushed cheeks pale, and his face became intent.

When she simply stared back into his eyes, her breathing fast and uneven, he muttered under his breath and lifted her close into his arms, his mouth covering hers.

Shock-waves of pleasure hit her, racing through her whole body in an instant, softening her as his arms gathered her up, pulled her tightly against him as he felt her delicately feminine response. She forgot everything. She was not ashamed, not embarrassed. Her only desire was to drown in him, never to surface, and she allowed herself to sink into a fantasy of swirling colour and light, clinging to him, her lips fused with his, time moving backwards to that first kiss, a kiss she had pushed out of her mind for months.

A small sound of protest murmured in her throat, although her slim arms wound around Jaime's neck, and for a second his kiss deepened, became all-consuming, possessive and fierce, so that she was bewildered when he suddenly pulled away.

They stared at each other like enemies, as indeed they were, but neither moved, and his eyes began a slow journey over her face, examining every detail as she stood there trembling.

'Did you think that was William, or did you know it was me?' he asked drily, suddenly snapping back to life, his dark eyes narrowed and sardonic.

'Why did you do it?' Sara asked breathlessly, not yet in control of her heartbeat.

'Why did you let me?' he countered softly. His hand came round her nape, his thumb tilting her face. 'I too have plans, *señorita*,' he informed her quietly. 'Perhaps you fit in with them.'

Magic vanished as temper flared, and Sara stepped clear of temptation, frowning ferociously at him, irritated further when he laughed softly.

'You are like an angry child,' he assured her. 'Get a little rest and keep that rage under strict control when you come down for dinner. Remember that I knew you in London, that we are good friends and that I am taking you to your father—when you are well!'

'I'm well now, and I'll tell them that, too!' Sara snapped.

'You have a little more colour than you had a few minutes ago,' he agreed, his hand stroking down her heated face, 'but when we came in to the house you were distinctly pale, obviously unfit to travel. I cannot promise to keep kissing you back to a healthy appearance. You might easily forget about William—and so might I!'

He strode from the room before she could draw breath to get back at him, and, after all, she was glad to take off her dress and creep into bed. One session with him and she felt emotionally drained. He was too dangerous to oppose, he used unfair methods of attack. She could still feel those hard, sensuous lips on hers as she fell asleep.

She hated him! Her mind told her that firmly, but her whole being, her soul even, had reacted to his kiss. The beauty of her feelings only slowly faded, like a shining thread of light that still lingered when darkness was complete.

She had felt safety in his arms for a second, safety and peace and a growing wonder, but her mind refused even to consider it, this foolish and dangerous flare of attraction. It could make her even more vulnerable. She went to sleep, deeply troubled, but her dreams were of hard, warm lips that she still felt searching hers.

Conchita awakened her as the day was fading into a deep blue evening, bringing her a steaming cup of tea and announcing that she was going to prepare a bath.

Later, dressed for the confrontation with the two women she had seen so briefly, Sara made her way slowly down the old dark stairs. With Conchita's help, she had chosen a dress of deep blue that picked up the colour of her eyes and made her hair shine like a glittering cloud of light around her head. It had been brushed repeatedly by Conchita, in spite of her protests, and she had been made a little uneasy by the old Mexican woman's frequent chuckles of amusement as she had plied the stiff brush through the thick amber hair.

Now, though, she pushed all other thoughts from her mind as she approached the closed door of the *sala* where Conchita had assured her they would all be waiting. Tonight, she intended to be calm and assured, ignoring the attitude of Constanza Carreras and María-Teresa. If need be, she would ignore Jaime, too.

Nevertheless, her determination took a severe jolt when she opened the door to find them waiting for her. It was one thing to imagine them, but quite another to see three pairs of dark eyes turned to her as she entered the room.

'Conchita said that I would find you here.' To gain a few minutes, she turned away to close the door, and when she turned back Jaime was beside her, taking her arm and drawing her forward.

'And you have found us. Good! Now we wait only for Hernando, and we will eat.' The incident in the bedroom earlier might never have happened. Sara could not help searching his face for some sign of his thoughts, but he was back to normal; dark, enigmatic and powerfully sure of himself. 'Meanwhile, I have news for you. I have arranged for you to call England. There is often some delay with these long-distance calls, and I have booked a call for you just after dinner if that is convenient for you?'

'Oh! Well, yes...' Sara tried not to let any of her surprise or anxiety show itself to the two women who stood watching with close interest. 'I—I'm very grateful!'

'Not at all!' he said, with all the arrogance she had begun to expect. 'After all, William will be "champing at the bit"!'

There was censure, sarcasm and a certain threatening air about him that had her instantly flushing, and she would have liked to walk out there and then.

'There is a man in the *señorita's* life already?' To Sara's surprise, the face of María-Teresa lost its petulance and took on a gleam of friendly interest, her eyes actually warming as Sara blushed helplessly.

'Why, yes, Sara has a great friend in England who—shares her life to some extent,' Jaime said goadingly. 'He worries about her!' he added with a wry look at Sara's face. He was needling her, even though he had warned her about bursts of temper.

'He cares about me and he's very kind!' she said to María-Teresa with a confiding look, one woman to another, ignoring Jaime's words and his twisted smile.

The remark had the unexpected effect of wiping the smile off Jaime's face.

'And he is very indulgent!' he snapped. 'Perhaps he will have reached the end of his indulgence when he realises exactly where you are! He cannot think so greatly of you if he is prepared to allow you to wander about alone in Mexico. Perhaps he was glad to see you go?'

'Jaime! What a thing to say!' Constanza Carreras murmured in a shocked voice. 'The *señorita* is quite beautiful, most unusual, and though you may not see it yourself, her friend no doubt does. After all, just because the Mexican male seems to prefer dark-haired women, there is no reason to suppose that Englishmen do so. I would think that when she is stronger she will fly off rapidly to her own country. Undoubtedly the young man there is pining for her this very minute, wondering where she is. It is a sad thought.'

'Extremely sad!' Jaime muttered between clenched white teeth. 'I am desolate at the idea!'

The whole conversation was astonishing. The fact that Jaime had spoken so openly before these two women was in itself surprising when he had worked out the attitude she was to take. It was obvious that, whatever his plans, she annoyed him too much for him to hold his tongue. Why she should have expected anything different, she did not know.

The thought, too, of William worrying was upsetting, and momentary distress showed on Sara's face. Jaime's booking of the telephone call had given her a feeling of gratitude, but in view of his attitude now she felt alarm. It was so out of character! What was he up to? Did he intend to stop her at the last minute? She felt tears of anxiety and frustration at the back of her eyes, and María-Teresa noticed at once.

'You are upsetting the *señorita*, Jaime!' she said quietly. 'You should not bring back such memories of this man when she has been away for so many weeks.'

'She will soon be able to speak to him!' Jaime's voice was indifferent to any upset. 'Meanwhile, you may leave Sara to me!'

'And to the man in England!' María-Teresa said with a little smile that earned her a glare. Evidently he had tired of the game he was playing.

'Can I really telephone England?' Sara asked in a whisper as the two women moved away, either tiring of the conversation or uneasy about Jaime's now tight face.

'I have already booked the call!' he said sharply, adding with a cruel sarcasm, 'Do not be so surprised, Sara. I have merely booked a call, not a flight. You are still here, right under my hand, well within reach.'

'If you imagine that I'll...' she began in a furious whisper, but her words died in her throat as he looked at her slowly and levelly.

'Yes,' he said softly, 'I imagine that you will, if you think that there is any advantage to be gained by it. However, as I told you in your room when you clung to me so ardently, it is not a good idea. We should try to remember William.'

Sara's face flared with colour, but she did not have the chance to reply because there was suddenly no quiet privacy. The door opened and she had her first glimpse of Hernando Riera, Jaime's secretary—and a very different atmosphere entered the room.

CHAPTER FIVE

'I HAVE not, I hope, kept you waiting?' Hernando's eyes were on Sara, on her bright hair and fair skin, and there was a heightening of the tension in the room, the petulance coming back to María-Teresa's face, and a further stiffening of Jaime's attitude.

'You are not late, Hernando,' he said coolly. 'Allow me to introduce you to Señorita Sara Lawrence. She will be here for a while, I imagine, so you will be able to get better acquainted at a later date.'

'Your servant, *señorita*.' Hernando Riera bowed and smiled. 'I am delighted that you are here. I shall spend every spare moment with you in future.'

The laughter in his voice took any spice from the remark, but María-Teresa did not appreciate this at all, and neither, it seemed, did Constanza Carreras.

Sara did not know whether Jaime was amused or not when he said sardonically, 'Remind me to double your workload. For now, let us eat, or Conchita will appear and scold us all.'

In spite of his attitude, however, Sara found herself seated next to Hernando and facing Jaime, the latter being at once fully occupied by María-Teresa, who started an animated conversation and twice had to be reminded to speak in English. She seemed to be intent upon keeping her eyes away from Sara and Hernando Riera. Not that it mattered. Sara was not listening to any conversation. Her mind was noting, as her eyes had noted, that twice at least Jaime's strong hand had covered the more slender fingers of his stepsister, and the action had been secret and lingering.

He apparently thought it was quite all right to kiss her in the bedroom and hold hands with his stepsister a few hours later. This was a type of morality that Sara found disgusting. He had been nasty and sarcastic earlier, and now there was no sign on his face that he even remembered. He was neither looking at her nor avoiding her glance, and she had to strive really hard to answer the questions that Hernando put to her. She was filled with anger at Jaime's attitude, and had misgivings as to whether she would be able to telephone, after all.

Hernando Riera was a very charming man, and she guessed that he was about twenty-six or -seven. Like his powerful employer, he was dark-haired, and in his own way very handsome, but his eyes had not the black brilliance of Jaime's, and her overall impression was of gentleness and kindness. The overall impression of Jaime was and would always be that of a vibrant force, an elemental power. Who could compare in any way? She had the dreadful feeling that he was invincible.

She realised belatedly that she was staring at him, and that both María-Teresa and Constanza were watching her. Jaime, too, had his eyes on her, his gaze narrowed thoughtfully.

'I'm sorry,' she said quickly. 'Were you speaking to me?'

'Merely a remark,' he assured her. 'Constanza asked how you had managed while in hospital for the things that you needed, and I said that you had everything that you needed at the moment, more than you seem to require.'

'Jaime bought things for me,' Sara confessed with a faint flush of colour. 'I have plenty of clothes, it seems.

More than I'm going to wear,' she added pointedly for his benefit.

She felt a shiver of apprehension as Jaime smiled wryly at this remark. She knew that her wardrobe contained enough clothes for an almost permanent stay here, and so did he. After all, he had bought them!

'Surely one cannot have too many clothes?' Constanza said with the air of one addressing a lunatic. 'You are without your usual amount of things, I'm sure!'

'Oh, there are one or two things that I would have normally had besides the things that Jaime bought me,' Sara said brightly, 'but I've never had such expensive clothes. It's something that I've never been able to afford. Few people are as rich as Jaime!'

His eyebrows raised quizzically, and she left him to make of that whatever he liked.

'Well, I'm sure that Jaime has enjoyed looking after you and getting expensive things for you. All this will be a novelty to him. It will be something for him to re-member with amusement when you go.'

'Yes, I expect it will,' Sara said, smiling sweetly at him. 'In a few days we shall be going to find my father. Has Jaime told you that he has promised to take me into the mountains to search for my father?'

His look of narrow-eyed warning was ignored as she ploughed on determinedly.

'If I hadn't had that stupid accident, I expect we should have already been there where my father is. We shall have to go very soon now though, because I have a job to get back to. I only have a little leave.' Actually, her leave was now up, and she could quite imagine Mr Partridge's face when she failed to turn up for work.

She wondered if Jaime was enjoying the game now that she had the ball. A quick look at his hostile face assured her that he was not. She didn't particularly care. If she could tie him up in knots, she would do so. She could imagine Constanza's daily questions in the future about the trip. She had not one single doubt that both women wanted her out of here as fast as possible.

'Yes, your father!' Constanza said with great enjoyment. 'He was once so very famous. I used to hear about him all the time!'

Sara stiffened, all the assumed sweetness dying from her face. Her mother used to hear about him all the time too, hear about his exploits, even when she had no wish to be hurt further. Her grandmother used to delight in reading the paper out loud to them at breakfast time if any news of Hector Lawrence was there. She would sit regally at the head of the table—*her* table—and deliver the news in a tone that would have been better used in a parliamentary debate. The 'morning press conference', her mother called it!

'I am astonished that he simply disappeared,' Constanza went on. 'Perhaps now he will come out and have a great find to show the world. And you are going to seek him! It is most exciting.'

'It's sheer necessity,' Sara said briefly, bitterness making tight lines around her mouth. 'Now that I'm well, I want to get it over with and get back to England!'

'Ah! Of course! You have this wonderful man there who will be waiting for you!' Constanza said smugly.

'Yes,' Sara assured her with a brief smile. 'William will be rather desperate to see me. There is no harshness, no arrogance in William.'

Her eyes were misty as she thought of William and his utter goodness. She avoided Jaime's eyes, but his stillness as he digested this whiplash was almost audible. She saw him put down his knife and fork with slow deliberation, but she refused to look up, and Constanza helped by blurting out her next question.

'But why are you doing this alone, Señorita Lawrence? At one time your father was always in the magazines. I thought that he was a lord, one of your English aristocracy, or something.'

'You shouldn't believe all that you read in the glossy magazines, *señora*,' Hernando was foolish enough to point out, and he earned himself a sharp look of reproof for speaking out of turn. Apparently Constanza was not so liberal as to appreciate the remarks of Jaime's secretary when she was hunting for information.

'My grandmother had the title, Señora Carreras,' Sara said quietly, 'but it was only a life peerage, for her political work. She died earlier this year, and left my father a considerable fortune. Of course, he doesn't know. I'm here to tell him the news. There was nobody else to come.'

'How very interesting!' Constanza was soaking in this information. 'You must miss your grandmother very much.'

'Not really,' Sara said softly. 'I hated her. Excuse me, please. I'm afraid I feel faint!' She left the table quickly and stepped out into the cooler air of the veranda, walking away, across the patio and into the darkened gardens.

The mention of her grandmother had upset her more than she had thought possible. All the old bitterness had come flooding back. If there was any obsession in her, then it was with this hatred, this blame she placed at the feet of her grandmother and her father. She walked further, staring blindly ahead, her mind far away in England, seeing her grandmother's autocratic face.

Her father had left them in his mother's care when Sara was small, promising to be back soon, assuring them of his love, secure in the knowledge that his mother would care for his wife and child, leaving his responsibilities behind him.

But Sylvia Lawrence had disliked her famous son's wife, for the very sweet and ordinary girl was not the sort of person she would have chosen for him, and her greatest pleasure was to humiliate her. Sara had been too young then to realise it, but she had realised it later, when it was almost too late...

Her son's wife was left out of anything that took place at the grand house, treated with veiled contempt by her grandmother when guests were there. Sara was brought in and paraded with satisfaction, as her grandmother pointed out the child's likeness to Hector, and how very little of her mother there was in her. She was quite secure in her many small cruelties and snubs. Hector had left nothing for his wife and child, relying on his mother's beneficence.

The things that her grandmother did for her had been done solely as an added twist to the knife that she held at the throat of her mother. Riding lessons, music lessons—anything that she could come up with to tie Sara to her and separate her from her mother. Sara's mother had known full well that she would have to leave before her own child was turned into a mirror image of the old woman.

She had left, taking Sara, working to keep them and hoping every day that her husband would return. He had not and, finally, even his letters had stopped, letters that had never once answered her mother's pleas for his return. It was too late now, her mother was dead, dead before her grandmother, worn out with work and grief, but all the bitterness and anger remained.

Jaime caught her as she stepped out under the trees, his hand coming tightly to her arm.

'I warned you of walking in the dark without me!' he said harshly. 'You seem to have no sense of danger!'

Sara simply turned back to the house and he let her walk, keeping his hand tightly on her, swinging her to face him when they came back within the circle of light.

'I hope that Constanza did not upset you,' he said, looking at her closely as the light caught her face, leaving his in the shadow.

'No!' She stared straight ahead and he watched her with narrowed eyes.

'You never told me about this grandmother,' he said quietly.

'Why should I have? I didn't know you! I didn't want to know you! I only asked for your help, and you refused. The rest of the chasing has been your own idea. *I* don't want you in my life, so why should I tell you my life history?'

He seemed stunned, although he should not have been. She had already demonstrated her ability to hit back hard when under threat. It didn't matter, anyway! The bitterness was back, as bad as ever, more strong now that she was in this land.

Some of William's words came back to her. They had quarrelled violently before she'd left. He was afraid for her, and it had made him speak out as he would never have done ordinarily.

'Do you realise, Sara, that your mother was not always ill?' he'd said. 'Couldn't she have left that old witch long before she did? She wasn't what the old lady wanted, but she wasn't stupid. *I* remember her. I'm older than you are, and one thing I do remember, she liked to whinge!'

The words had hit Sara like a blow. It was true that her mother had complained to her even when she was quite small, and maybe she should not have done that, but Sara had seen her mother become ill, had seen her die! If her grandmother had not behaved as she had done, then her mother would have been able to live more easily. She would have been alive today!

She had told William that forcefully, but he had been unrepentant.

'There was no need for her to leave, Sara! She only needed to stand up to the old lady and give as good as she got! She preferred to complain though, to you, even when you were small and easily swayed. Your father wasn't too powerful, either. He just went off and did his thing like a schoolboy, with no thought for anything else. You stand up to everything and everybody. You've more of the old lady in you than you think!'

That was when Sara had walked out of the house and bought her ticket to Mexico. Now she wondered if she should have listened, talked to him, explained that he had not been there to see! She missed him. He was the only firm peg in her life.

Sara didn't even know that she was crying bitterly until two arms came around her. She had completely forgotten Jaime in her grief-stricken thoughts. She jerked her head away from his shoulder, where it seemed to be resting, but he pulled it gently back.

'Ssh! Be still!' he said quietly. 'I do not know what storm Constanza has called up, but it must blow itself out before you face them again.'

'I—I'm perfectly all right!' Sara said tightly, as stiff as a rod in his arms, unable to get free.

'I am sure that you are,' he said with laughter in his deep voice, 'but please, stay and be perfectly all right here for a while.'

He was quietly kind and she succumbed to the temptation, resting against him and finishing her burst of misery against the comfortable warmth of his shoulder.

When her unhappiness had subsided, Sara felt embarrassed and very annoyed with herself. As he felt her stiffen, Jaime released her and led her back into the house. She was pleased to see that dinner was over and that the two women had retired to the *sala* to play cards with Hernando.

María-Teresa heard them come in, apparently, because she appeared at the door of the dining-room, begging Jaime to join them. Although he refused, saying that he must assist with the expected phone call, he did not refuse in any unpleasant way, and his eyes still smiled at María-Teresa until she closed the door behind her, her face flushed and smiling. She had entirely ignored the signs of tears on Sara's face, and Sara was grateful for that. She was recovered now, and she wanted neither sympathy nor questions.

Jaime led Sara to the study and then simply sat on the edge of the desk, waiting with great patience that only added to Sara's mounting nervousness. He said nothing at all, and when the telephone call was finally arranged, he walked out of the room after handing the receiver to her with no comment whatsoever.

William seemed to be almost beside her, the line was so clear, but even knowing Jaime's great wealth she felt the need to hurry with this call, for the expense of it alarmed her.

'Sara!' William was astonished to hear from her. 'Are you back in England? You sound to be almost in the same room!'

'No, I—I'm still in Mexico. William, I'm...'

'Don't say it, Sara,' he interrupted warmly. 'I'm the one to be sorry. I should never have said what I did. I know how you feel.'

'I hate to quarrel with you!' Sara burst out, and his voice was soothing, even from so far off.

'I hate it too, love. Never again. Well, did you find him?' he asked, with a certain amount of excitement and no anger at all.

There was something to be happy about, after all. William had forgiven her for her headstrong decision to rush off to Mexico; he was only interested in her news and getting her back.

'No—no, er—I haven't been able to get on with it. I—I had an accident...'

He exploded into sound, anxious and angry at the same time, and she had to raise her voice to stop him.

'I'm all right, William, truly I am,' she said urgently. 'I've been in hospital and now I'm out and I'm all right.'

It was difficult to tell him that she had survived a plane crash and was still in one piece, but after a while he was convinced.

'So where are you now?' he asked firmly. There was no nonsense about William.

'I—I'm staying with—friends,' she said warily.

'Where?' It came to her mind that William was standing there with a notebook and pen, preparing to write her address and come out here to get her. If only he could!

'It's in the mountains. I don't know exactly the place but, William, I'll try to ring you again and let you know then...' About to say that he could come for her, Sara suddenly looked up and saw Jaime as he stood leaning against the open door. All her instincts rose up to protect William. Her eyes roamed over the tall physical perfection that was Jaime Carreras, and she saw William's lameness, their lack of money, lack of the language. He was safer at home!

'Then you can write to me,' she finished futilely, and saw Jaime's eyebrows raise sardonically.

Her voice lowered to huskiness as she answered William's demand to know when she was coming back.

'I—I don't know when I'll be back, William,' she said quietly. 'As soon as I find him. I miss you!' she finished rather plaintively, not wanting at all to lose her contact with home, but it was time.

After that, her departure from the study could not be quick enough, but Jaime waylaid her, taking her arm and swinging her towards him.

'I have not yet taken you to task for attempting to land me in trouble at dinner tonight,' he said evenly. 'It surely proves that I am not as barbaric as you suppose, when I allow you to get away with recounting promises that I did not make, and then hold you in my arms when you are upset!'

'Thank you for your kindness!' Sara said firmly, pulling her arm away. 'As to the promises, you stated quite clearly that you intended to take me to my father!'

'But not, as you led all to believe, with much alacrity!' he pointed out coolly. 'It will be much longer than you think before I take you into the mountains.'

'Look! I can't wait so long!' Sara said, moving closer to him in her exasperation, her face raised as she tried to make him see some sense. 'Some of us have jobs to go to in places that we do not own! If I'm away much longer, I just will not have a job to back to. People in the banking world are expected to be reliable! Surely you can understand that? You seem to own a bank yourself!'

'I wonder, *señorita*, just how stupid you imagine I am,' he said with a slight smile. 'There is not much chance of your bank having given you as much leave as you have taken, not someone in your position!'

'Oh, I know that I'm very lowly!' Sara snapped. 'There's really no need to point it out!'

'I am not doing that at all,' he remarked calmly. 'I am speculating and coming to the conclusion that you have already lost your job at the bank. It does not matter, surely? The man was an ogre, as you told me.'

'People put up with lots of things in order to eat!' Sara reminded him, and he smiled more widely.

'But I will not let you starve, Sara. Stay here with me. Have a nice long holiday. I will take you to see your father much later and when we come back—we will see.'

'Do they know?' Sara snapped viciously. 'Do your family and your secretary know that you're offering me a new position? Is that why María-Teresa looks at me and sulks?'

'She is jealous,' he admitted, his eyes roaming over her, 'but I keep my private affairs to myself.'

'Well, I do not intend to be a private affair of yours! I'd fight you with every last breath!' Sara said furiously, her face flushed and angry.

'As you did in your room when I kissed you? As you did not long ago in the garden when I held you in my arms?' he asked drily. 'If I recall, *señorita*, it was I who pulled away from the kiss!'

There was no answer to that, and Sara swept out of the room with what she hoped was some dignity.

It was very much later, when Sara still paced her darkened room, her mind turning things over and over, that she stepped out on to the balcony, utterly disregarding Jaime's warning. She came to a sudden stop, feeling unspeakably guilty when she heard voices just below on the patio, and she was afraid to move, glad that the light was out in her room. She felt like an eavesdropper. It was Jaime and María-Teresa.

'But what are we going to do, Jaime?' the girl was saying. 'Mama will never agree to the marriage.'

'It is up to you to make her agree, *querida*,' Jaime said, his arms coming around her. 'What is the sense in this frustration, in this waiting? You know how I feel about it! Tell her that you will do as you like and you will make two people very happy.'

Sara saw the girl's pale face tilted for a kiss, and then María-Teresa went into the house. Jaime stood there for a moment longer, leaning on the rail, his eyes on the darkened garden, and Sara stealthily withdrew into her room.

He had held Sara in his arms, kissed her, offered to be her—her lover! All the time he was planning to marry his stepsister! She felt utterly stunned, and realised the depths of his scorn for her, the little regard he had for her character. If he did not promise at once to take her to her father, she would find another way, even if it meant telling the girl about his wicked deceit!

CHAPTER SIX

IN THE morning there was no sign of Jaime, and Sara felt extremely fretful. Another day wasted! She wandered around the house in the hope of meeting him and being able to bring up the subject of her trip again, but she finally reached the conclusion that he was out somewhere. There was no advantage to be gained by that, even. She was still without papers of any kind, without money, and she did not even know with any accuracy exactly where she was.

It was with a feeling of growing frustration that she eventually searched among the brand-new clothes in her room and came up with a dark blue bikini. She might at least get a tan out of this!

It was hot by the pool, but she determinedly sought the brightest place and stretched out to enjoy the sun. She closed her eyes, lying back on the lounger and letting the hot sunshine ease her limbs and her mind. The beauty of the place was breathtaking. It was a land of flowers. The mountains soared in the distance, spectacular, grand and alarming; the air was like wine. Anyone should be happy here in this tranquillity, anyone but Sara Lawrence. There was no tranquillity in her mind.

'*Señorita?*' The softly spoken word roused her sufficiently to have her attention, and she opened her eyes to find Hernando Riera watching her.

'I am sorry!' he said regretfully. 'I did not know whether you were awake or asleep. I had hoped that perhaps you were simply resting, and now I have disturbed you.'

'It's all right!' She sat up and managed a smile for him. If she was to have a friend at all here, then the only one she could think of was Hernando. He was the pilot, too. Maybe he would help her to escape? Jaime's face came into her mind, and she dismissed that unlikely idea at once. Nobody would risk Jaime's anger, and Hernando's next words confirmed it.

'I have transgressed very seriously,' he confessed with a shrug. 'Jaime has given orders that you are to be allowed to rest. Here I am disturbing you on your first day of resting!'

'You're not disturbing me at all. I was only lying with my eyes closed for a second,' Sara said quickly. Why the particular order had been given, she did not know. Probably the fewer people she spoke to when Jaime was not there meant there was a better chance that the true state of affairs would not come out. It was lucky for him that she was satisfied to allow this state of things to continue for the moment. Unless something better came up!

'Do sit and talk to me for a while, Señor Riera,' she said with all the charm she could muster. It wasn't too difficult with this man. There was nothing alarming about him. Probably Jaime had driven any spirit out of him!

'Hernando, please!' he said with a smile, sitting opposite her. 'Great formality makes me uneasy.' He leaned back and smiled, looking so relaxed that his next remark caught her off guard. 'How well do you know Jaime?' he asked carelessly, his eyes on the distant mountain range.

'Not too well. He—he was in England quite recently, as you know, and...well, we had a mutual acquaintance, that's all.' She tried to be flippant about it, but he had caught the unease in her voice and turned to look closely at her.

'Sorry, I appear to be prying. It is hard to believe that you know him very slightly when he is so intense about you.'

'I expect he's a very intense man.' Sara laughed uneasily. 'I'm grateful for his—kindness.'

'I have never noticed intensity among his characteristics until last night at dinner,' Hernando said softly. 'He has the reputation of being utterly cold and calm. He is quite famous, as I suppose you know, famous without requiring such an honour. He is a very private man—solitary, in actual fact. He inherited a great deal of wealth. His family have been merchant bankers for generations, and now this is all in Jaime's hands. He deals with everything calmly and methodically. I have never known him show very much emotion except, perhaps, anger. Last night, however, when you retired early, he was—greatly disturbed, very quiet.'

'I expect that I'm a burden,' Sara said sharply. She suddenly didn't want to discuss Jaime like this. She had the ridiculous feeling that she was being treacherous. She did not want to have anyone prying into her affairs, either, and she had the distinct feeling that Hernando Riera was doing just that. In any case, she knew why Jaime had been silent and disturbed. It was nothing to do with her at all. It was his frustration at not being able to marry María-Teresa straight away. Why Constanza was opposing it was a mystery. He was wealthy beyond imagination, as far as she had been able to gather. In any case, it was none of her business. He

only concerned her as far as he was an interfering and
irritating block in her attempts to get to her father. She
had problems enough, without any interrogation, and
her tight frown brought a smile to Hernando's lips.

'I am prying like a woman!' he confessed with a laugh.
'I admit to being intrigued. Mysteries always fascinate
me, and you are quite mysterious, Sara. During your
stay in hospital he has not strayed too far afield. He has
responsibilities and he fulfils them rigorously. I take
much of the work off his hands, and of course there are
others who also do that, but there are times when only
he can make decisions and then he must be there.' He
eyed her ruefully. 'Sometimes he is not there, and then
there are moments of panic in the banking world. I have
dealt with the panics while you have been in Mexico. For
the first time ever, to my knowledge, he has delegated
great responsibility and stayed right here. As I say, I am
intrigued!'

'Perhaps he's training you for greater things!' Sara
said a little sarcastically. Hernando Riera was just too
near to the truth for her liking, and it was alarming, to
say the least, to discover that Jaime had neglected everything to be close when she was in hospital. Why he had
done that was no mystery to her. He had neglected his
own affairs, it seemed, in order to interfere with hers!
'He's a very unusual man,' Sara added quietly. 'Frightening, sometimes.'

'I can only agree,' Hernando said drily. 'Not however,
as frightening as Señora Carreras!'

'Why do you say that?' Sara asked, intrigued herself,
and only too glad to change the subject.

'She is a woman with cast-iron plans, and a will to
match!' he said briefly, and Sara was amused to find
that she was not about to get any more information from

him than he had received from her. It was like a very
polite game of chess. A draw seemed to have been
declared.

'I wanted to ask you something,' she said as non-
chalantly as possible. 'How far are we from any good-
sized town?'

'An awkward question,' he said with a laugh. 'It depends you what you mean. We are close enough to a
town to get supplies if we need them, but nowhere near
to what you would perhaps call civilisation, coming as
you do from the capital city of your country. We are
between the mountains and the sea, quite a long way
from each of them. I suppose that the nearest place that
would be acceptable to you would be Mexico City itself.
It depends upon what you want.'

Escape! Sara thought wryly. She had expected as
much. There was no way of getting out of here without
help, and a close look at Hernando, at his sharp, intelligent eyes, told her that she had better watch her tongue.
He would be firmly on Jaime's side. Not only did his
job depend on it, but he was treated like one of the
family.

Perhaps similar thoughts had been going through his
head, because he stood almost abruptly and bowed a
small, almost ironical bow.

'I really must get on before Jaime comes and demands
an explanation of this dalliance,' he said pleasantly, and
she was startled but greatly relieved that he went at once.

The reason for this departure soon became clear:
Jaime's great black car came sweeping up the drive and
stopped at the side of the house. Evidently Hernando
had heard the gates. She had not, but the look in Jaime's
dark eyes as he came with deceptive casualness around

to the pool told her that he had seen the speedy departure.

'I see that you have not been lacking company,' he said drily, his eyes skimming over her slender figure. 'I am not surprised!'

'I expect you bought the bikini!' she said with an instant rise of aggression at the veiled scorn. 'I could have sunbathed in a long fur coat, but there wasn't one in my wardrobe!'

'What did he want?' he asked sharply, ignoring her sarcasm. 'I gave orders that you were not to be disturbed.'

'And he was suitably contrite!' Sara said sweetly. 'Don't worry, he was only making general conversation, and I didn't beg him to fly me out of here!'

'What a wasted opportunity!' he mocked. 'I would have thought that gaining an ally would be the first thought in your mind, and it would have been so easy for you. After all, he's a man!'

'I don't need allies!' she said angrily. 'I just need action! If you're only here to insult me, then I'll not even reply!'

She closed her eyes, leaning back, her body trembling with suppressed annoyance, and she heard his mutter of exasperation. He got up and walked over to her, but she ignored him, although there was a quick, frightening feeling of awareness even though her eyes were shut.

'You still have bruises on your head,' he said tightly. 'You were badly hurt.'

'Don't be sorry for me,' she managed sarcastically, opening her eyes and looking up at him. 'I'll be crying all over you.'

'If you feel the need.'

Her face flooded with colour as she remembered last night, and his eyes held hers until she quickly looked away.,

'What were you so deeply discussing with Hernando?' he suddenly shot at her, his voice back to harshness.

'We were talking about your great power, how everyone needs you. Surely he's trained to sing your praises?' She suddenly sat up frustratedly, swinging her legs to the ground, determined to walk off. 'We were talking about the country around here, if you really must know! And then, of course, I was checking up on your wealth!' she said bitterly, looking up at him with a show of spirit. 'I have to weigh one kind of future against the other!'

His smile was one of admiration, but he only spoke in a derisive tone.

'Even now, you are no further forward, are you? Hernando knows better than to discuss my affairs. Nevertheless, I hope that he spoke well of my prospects, my ability to take care of all your desires?'

His taunting voice was altogether too much, and she moved abruptly, getting to her feet, but he instantly blocked her retreat, his eyes shining intently into hers.

'I am making you agitated,' he said with little show of remorse. 'I did promise to treat you like an invalid for a while, but with you, it is difficult. You must forgive my lack of consideration.'

She looked up into his face, her eyes held by the black glitter of his gaze, her heart beginning to pound heavily at the way he watched her. He was silent, alert, an almost predatory gleam at the very back of his hypnotic eyes that was totally at variance with his polite and apologetic words.

'You have not offered to forgive me,' he pointed out in a deep, velvety murmur, frightening her even more as his gaze began to roam over her, his eyes shuttered under heavy lids.

'There is too much about you that is unforgivable,' she said quietly. 'I'm grateful that you rescued me, grateful for your efforts to get me to hospital, but there my gratitude stops. Left at the hospital alone I would have been handed over to the authorities, and by now I would be in England, having seen my father and settled all this completely!'

His hand slowly raised and reached out to touch her arm, to run tentatively up from her wrist to her shoulder, his eyes following the light, almost delicate movement of his brown fingers before returning to her troubled face.

'I have decided to take you myself,' he murmured, his hand continuing its light exploration of her skin, moving now to the silken smoothness of her neck. His eyes were amused when she pulled away sharply. 'Do not be alarmed, Sara. You may take that remark at its face value,' he murmured.

His hands suddenly moved to encircle her waist and urge her forward.

'If I keep you here for ever, though, who is to know, except William?'

'You—you're trying to frighten me! You can't do that! You haven't enough power to get away with any of the things you keep threatening!' She said it with an attempt at derision, but her lips were trembling and his eyes snapped to their tremulous beauty.

'Oh, I am well aware that you think I am a wealthy *bandido*,' he murmured. 'But you are excited. Every time you are near me, you are excited. You want me to kiss you, to hold you close to me.' His hand moved to cradle her head, lifting her face to his. 'You do not really wish to be protected from me.'

'I don't want you to *touch* me!' she said frantically.

'But you do, Sara,' he breathed. 'Your mind fights me, protests, but your body knows its own needs.'

'No!' Her face flushed with a mixture of fear and excitement that he had so astutely recognised. 'I don't need anything. I just want to get to my father and then go home!'

She was making no attempt to pull away, and his dark eyes acknowledged the fact with satisfaction, his hands moving her ever closer.

'I do not wish you to go,' he reminded her softly. 'I like things exactly as they are for now. A softly pliant girl in my arms, with no thoughts but desire in her mind.'

'It's not true!' She tried to move, but she had left it too late and his firm lips hovered over hers.

'Let us see,' he said quietly. 'Let us find out what it is that is making you so uneasy.'

At first it was a kiss as light as thistledown, quiet and comforting, but, as her tight muscles relaxed beneath the gentle onslaught, his kiss deepened, taking her by surprise, forcing the feelings back that she had felt before, this desire to drown in his arms. She sighed softly against his mouth, her body eager when he pulled her towards him.

His hands moved over the smooth skin of her back, arching her against him as her fingers slowly uncurled and lay passively against his chest, her legs against the strength of his own as he moved his lips to her neck and the tender curve of her chin, his hands coaxing and possessive on her hips. 'One thing you cannot pretend,' he murmured, his eyes vibrant on her face as he lifted his head at last. 'You want me!'

For a moment they simply looked into each other's eyes, all time suspended as his gaze ran over her beautiful, flushed face.

'What a pity that you are capable of looking like this and being someone entirely different inside. What should I do? Should I enjoy you as you seem to be, take what I want, or should I remember that you are merely a dream creature, a girl who is not at all as she looks, a girl with plans for her future who will let nothing stop her? Shall we continue to play this game? Or should I remember the truth and look at you with different eyes?'

'What am I, Jaime?' she cried bitterly, strangely hurt. 'You don't know me at all!'

'You are Sara,' he said harshly, 'with hair like the sun, eyes like the evening skies. Sara, who is magic in my arms. Sara, with nothing but greed in her heart!'

His head swooped to hers and his lips found their goal relentlessly, deep desire in his kiss, and her own lips opened beneath his, eagerness in the whole of her body, in spite of everything she was unable to resist.

He was abominable and she was worse! She knew that he was going to marry his stepsister, and she had no doubts about her hatred for him. It was just this terrifying need to be in his arms!

She pulled away from him, running from the pool and into the house, racing to her own room with a speed that made her legs tremble and her heart pound. He was right, she was utterly vulnerable whenever he held her. It was a weakness he would exploit to the full as he amused himself during her stay here. She could so easily be ensnared, and he knew it. She did not even like him at all, but she was lost whenever he touched her. Somehow she had to get away before she simply stayed here just to be with him.

She showered quickly, meaning to rest before dinner, but, as she came in her robe from the shower, she found Constanza Carreras sitting in one of the armchairs in her room, waiting for her.

Ignoring Sara's look of surprise, she came straight to the point, apparently seeing no reason to hedge.

'I could not help seeing the little scene that took place by the pool, Señorita Lawrence,' she said tightly. 'I would like you to understand that I was not spying. It is not my place to spy on Jaime in his own house, but it was out in the open for anyone to see, even María-Teresa,' she added with annoyance. 'I cannot entirely blame you, *señorita*. Jaime is, after all, a man—and a handsome and rich one, accustomed to having his own way in everything. And as I have already said, you are a very beautiful girl. However, it is only fair to tell you that Jaime will marry María-Teresa as soon as she is twenty.'

Sara was stunned by the autocratically cold voice, but not by the announcement. Here then was the reason for so much frustration. Señor Carreras had two years to wait before he married his stepsister. She had seen how the girl looked at him, the way he smiled into her eyes. What was her own fate supposed to be, then, when he made her the constantly repeated offers? Was she to be a mistress, kept in the nearest city or some mountain lodge?

She believed Constanza Carreras. She had heard Jaime and the girl talking only last night. It also explained why María-Teresa had her eyes constantly on Sara, and why she was so much more friendly when the mention of a man in England had arisen.

'I'm quite sure that you have nothing to fear, Señora Carreras,' she said quietly. 'Jaime treats me only as a guest who is ill, and in any case, I have a life in England and someone waiting for me. I'm sure that you misunderstood what you saw. He is merely kind to me. I was upset and I know he doesn't like that. Please don't let it worry you.'

'Just how well did you know Jaime in England, Señorita Lawrence?' Constanza asked stiffly, knowing quite well what she had seen.

'Hardly at all,' Sara said with a dismissive smile. 'We had a mutual friend, that's all. It was just lucky for me that he had agreed to guide me to my father, and that he was the one who found me after the plane crashed.'

The effort brought her a beaming smile, and Constanza stood to leave, quite happy with her little chat.

'I'm so glad, my dear,' she smiled. 'I know that Jaime cannot be hurt. I was only thinking of you. The marriage was Jaime's father's very last wish. That is why we are still here. After all, I have a house in Mexico City that would suit me very much better than this outlying place.'

'You have no reason to worry about me,' Sara said with a stiff smile. 'In fact, I shall be going quite soon.'

'You are welcome to stay, of course,' Constanza Carreras said graciously. 'Do not feel that you must leave immediately, and of course you must find your father. I will be most interested in the outcome of that!'

Won't we all! Sara thought. So, he was intent upon amusing himself with her for a while, was he? She would lead him a fine dance! She suddenly sat down, her face worried. It wouldn't do at all. Encouraging him would lead to more than she could handle. He only had to reach

out and touch her and he had won. He already knew
that.

Over the next few days, it was all easily confirmed.
There was a deep sort of conspiracy between Jaime and
María-Teresa, their heads were together whenever they
thought that nobody was looking, although Constanza
was looking more often than not, like a preening
peacock, pleased with her offspring. She even nodded
knowingly in Sara's direction several times when their
eyes met, silently pointing out the truth of her remarks
in Sara's bedroom. She need not have bothered. Sara
was not blind, and her desire to escape reached a
crescendo.

Hernando, too, confirmed her knowledge. She met
him one day when she was wandering disconsolately in
the gardens and he fell into step beside her, seemingly
not too happy himself.

'Without wishing you to leave, Sara,' he said in a dis-
gruntled voice, 'I would be happy if Jaime returned to
his old habits of either being hard at it in the city or
simply off into the mountains with his friends the
Indians!'

'I'm not keeping him!' Sara protested. 'In any case,
I want to get to my father and then go home.'

'Apparently he does not think that you are fit to travel
yet,' Hernando said quietly, his glance skimming her
lovely face. 'Señora Carreras has mentioned it more than
once in my hearing. Jaime seems to think that the trip
would be too much for you at the moment, however. It
appears that you are also not well enough to be left while
he goes about his business, either!' he added grimly, his
eyes on her tanned face and healthy skin.

'Maybe he's too busy planning things with María-
Teresa,' Sara said against her will, her tongue intent upon

running away with her. 'It's a long time to their marriage if they have to wait until she's twenty, but they must have a lot to talk about. Maybe that's why he's still staying here. It seems to make Señora Carreras happy to see their heads constantly together.'

'Ah! She had told you, then? It is her life's work to unite those two!' Hernando said bitterly. 'If she succeeds, I will find another post. She is bad enough as a stepmother in this house, as a mother-in-law she will be unbelievable!'

The harsh bitterness of his voice surprised Sara. Constanza Carreras was perfectly pleasant to him as far as she knew. Still, she did not like it when Hernando talked to María-Teresa for too long; maybe, after all, she thought of him as a servant and was pleasant only for Jaime's sake. She would have more power as the bride's mother. She could see his point.

He left her soon after and Sara could let her guard down, allowing forbidden feelings to flow over her. She was jealous! Her mind fought against the idea, but she was too intelligent to be able to reject it. It was hateful of Jaime to kiss her and hold her, when he was going to marry that girl. It was hateful of her to let him!

She stopped beneath a flowering tree, leaning her head against it, fighting this latest problem, longing for the comfort of seeing William.

'Keep still!' Jaime's voice close by made her stiffen, but his tone held her still as a mouse, and he came to her swiftly, his hand flicking to her hair as he pulled her away from the tree.

'You take a great deal of watching!' he said with no humour. 'Even in England you would be likely to get something very nasty in your hair if you rested your head against a tree. Here, it could be anything from a snake to the giant bee that I have now despatched!'

'Oh!' Sara leapt away from the tree with a shudder, bumping into him, her hands to her hair.

'It is gone,' he assured her with a sudden laugh, his hands tightening on her too slender waist. 'Come, I have to go into the next village. I will take you with me and keep you out of mischief. You are much better, I think, and quite ready to be allowed out of the grounds.'

It sounded a little too much like a reference to prison, to Sara's mind, but she was all attention deep inside. She would be able to look around, get some idea of where she was, make some sort of plan to escape from Jaime.

He saw her face change and his smile was sardonic.

'I intend to keep on eye on you all the time,' he said drily. 'Also, it is a mountain village where nobody speaks English. If you are planning to fly from me, then the village will not be much use to you.'

'You know that all this is quite ridiculous, I suppose?' Sara said angrily, jerking herself away from his hands. 'I've been trapped here only because I want your help to get to my father! I could have well done without your idiotic threats to keep me here for ever!'

'You think that they were not real, *señorita*?' he said softly, watching her intently.

'*Real*?' Sara looked up at him with angry blue eyes, all thoughts of tears now gone. He was some sort of sadistic monster, or so besotted with his own power that he imagined he could do exactly as he liked. 'You can stop threatening me! I know that you're going to marry María-Teresa as soon as she is old enough! And another thing...'

'Old enough? My stepsister is old enough to marry now,' he said with a curious look at her. 'She is eighteen. Here, that is considered to be very mature, *señorita*.'

'For a peasant, perhaps!' Sara snapped. 'I'm quite sure that you feel the dignity of your position, and in any case, it was probably in your father's will!'

He began to laugh, a soft laugh deep in his throat that irritated her enough to have her glare at him with a dangerous light in her eyes. The light in his eyes was more dangerous, though.

'I would not advise violence, *señorita*!' he said in a deceptively quiet voice. 'You have succeeded in that twice, and I am not about to allow it again. As to María-Teresa, she is a delightful girl when she is not being jealous, but you are altogether more exciting. Not at all submissive. Handling you would be a trial and a pleasure.'

'You must be quite out of your mind!' Sara said scathingly. 'Are you seriously imagining that I would agree to live with you?'

'Why not?' he said derisively, his grip like iron. 'You are living with this William, why not with me?'

'But I *want* to live with William!' Sara said waspishly. 'I have never had any wish to live with you, Señor Carreras! Where would we live, as a matter of casual interest? In a hut in the mountains, where nobody would know about me?'

'It is more than likely!' he bit out angrily. 'I have not entirely given up the idea either, *señorita*!'

He looked so menacing that for a moment a thrill of fear raced down her spine, and he saw the fear reflected in her eyes.

'Oh, come along!' he snapped. 'Perhaps I am growing tired of you, after all! You are hardly a bright light in my life, with your unruly tongue and your greedy little mind. The trip to the village will blow some of the temper from you. It is a mountain road, and I know that will silence you!'

'I'm not going!' Sara said heatedly, pulling against his grip. 'The mountain road that I take out of here when I leave for ever will be more than enough to face!'

He simply lifted her struggling into his arms, walking angrily through the garden and dumping her unceremoniously into the Land Rover that stood in front of the house.

'Make a scene by trying to escape,' he snapped, 'and I will drive to this mountain hut you have fixed in your mind and settle your fate without more ado!'

It was enough to silence her, and she sat stonily as he walked round the vehicle to climb in.

'Jaime, can I come, too?' María-Teresa came running lightly from the house, her face hopeful as she stopped by Jaime to look up at him, and his arms instantly went around her.

'No, *querida*!' he said with a smile. 'I will not be long, and you know that there is nothing there to interest you. The road is rough and this vehicle is not the height of comfort. I would not want you to be tossed about.'

'No, that is true.' She smiled up at him and he gave her hair a playful little tug.

'I will take you and Constanza the very next time that I go to Mexico City. I know that you are sometimes bored here.'

'Not really, Jaime,' she said with a little knowing look at him, 'but I am always ready to fly with you anywhere.'

He smiled into her eyes and kissed her cheek, his lips lingering before he released her, and then he got in and drove off with one of those secret smiles they always seemed to give each other. Sara sat in silent misery, telling herself that she hated this arrogant and unkind man, but knowing that it was just not true.

CHAPTER SEVEN

THE ROAD was certainly rough and mountainous. The other road had been very alarming, clinging to the mountain wall, but this one was worse; it climbed steeply, twisting back on itself until it became apparent that nothing but a four-wheel-drive vehicle could have been used. It seemed to be leading nowhere, but suddenly the road straightened and they drove into a village that gave the impression of being perched in the clouds.

The whole place seemed to be golden, from the stone of the buildings to the sunlight that flooded the main square, and Jaime glanced quickly at Sara's entranced face as he came to help her out. They were instantly the focus of all eyes. Children stopped playing, the old men sitting with their drinks stopped talking and there was a buzz of excited chatter from the women who were washing clothes at the fountain that stood to the side of the square. It was quite clear to Sara that they were discussing her.

When Jaime took her hand to lead her across the dusty street, she made no move to free herself; instead she clung on tightly, her eyes downcast until he looked at her curiously.

'What is the matter?' he said softly. 'You are as nervous as a cat. You are quite safe. Maybe I have kept you isolated for too long, if the thought of walking across an ordinary village street alarms you.'

'It—it's the way they're looking at me,' she said uneasily. 'I *feel* nervous.'

112

He began to laugh softly, tucking her hand under his arm, his dark eyes glancing round at the villagers, who roused themselves sufficiently to smile and greet him politely.

'You are the only one here with a fair skin and blue eyes,' he said in amusement. 'Few, if any, English *señoritas* find their way here. Your hair is shining in the sunlight like a beacon, the colour of the sun itself. Naturally, they are intrigued.'

He walked her to the edge of the village and stopped as the land suddenly sheered away. There was a fence and then nothing, and Sara's breath caught in wonder as she looked out across the miles of countryside at the great panoramic view. Everything was on a grand scale: vistas of ochre rock rising from the valley floor, great mountain walls streaked with red strata and, down in the valley itself, the greenery of trees, the glitter of water and the brilliance of flowers. It was like a painting on a giant canvas, utterly stunning. Far in the distance, the mighty snow-capped volcano stood in imperious splendour against the blue sky.

'A land of flowers, mountains and high volcanoes!' she whispered almost to herself, realising for the first time that her feelings about this land were changing. She had few doubts as to why.

'Yes,' he said quietly, hearing no doubt some wistful strain to her voice. 'You are looking at a small corner of Mexico. What do you think of it?'

'My opinion could hardly be given without prejudice,' Sara said shortly. 'This land has brought me misery for as far back as I can remember. Nothing could change my thoughts about it!'

She turned away from the scene and he turned too, stiffly angry as he took her arm.

'A country does not bring misery, Sara!' he said tightly. 'It is the people in it who cause grief.'

'We're agreed on that!' she said briefly, and apparently he took her point.

'It is time for your appointment, anyway!' he said abruptly. 'The house is just at the edge of the main square.'

'What appointment?' The old feeling of panic rose at once, and she stopped in the middle of the road, facing him anxiously.

'You are to see the doctor for a check-up,' he said with an impatient look at her. 'It is time!'

'What doctor? Why didn't you tell me?' Sara asked suspiciously, her eyes intently on his cold face. 'The hospital isn't here! The doctor is at the hospital!'

'I imagine, *señorita*, that even in England doctors have a home, a place to lay their heads? The doctor from the hospital just happens to have his home here, and he has consented to see you at his house. It saves the longer journey to the hospital, and is a less alarming road, even though it is rough. And now that we have ascertained that this village is not the centre of a white slave ring, can we perhaps go on and keep the appointment?'

She felt her colour flare at his biting sarcasm and went meekly enough now. The business of the village had come to a halt again to watch this brief but angry exchange, and she was filled with embarrassment.

Jaime was clearly too annoyed to wait for her at the doctor's house, leaving her after a few words with the doctor and telling her sternly that he would wait for her across the square at the small café, and that she was to stand on the steps as she came out and wait to be collected. It made her feel like a parcel, and her temper rose as her fears subsided. It was the same doctor, though—there had been nothing to worry about.

The examination was thorough, and even she could tell that the doctor was satisfied with her recovery. Jaime strode across and went in to speak to him as she came out, leaving her standing in the shade of the veranda, and her heartbeats quickened when a big, brightly coloured camper rolled into the square, another treat for the isolated villagers and a ray of hope for her. She walked forward and was standing close by as the owners stepped out.

'Well, my goodness! Miles from anywhere and the first face we see is American!'

The soft American accent was like music to Sara's ears, and she smiled with pleasure at the middle-aged woman in checked shirt and jeans who came round to clasp her hand and pump it up and down.

'English!' she said with a laugh, turning to greet the man who came eagerly forward to introduce himself.

'Eddie Greenberg!' he said heartily. 'This is my wife Millicent. We're sure surprised to see you, little lady! What in the blazes are you doing here in this place?'

'Oh, I'm staying close by with—with friends,' Sara said quickly. 'How on earth did you manage to get that great big camper up here? The road we came on is impossible.'

'Is that a fact?' He shook his head. 'That's the end of that for a plan then, Millie!' he remarked to his wife. 'The road in from this direction is rough but quite level,' he added to Sara. 'It runs straight to the main highway. It's a climb, but nothing to be anxious about.'

'I think you'll end up rolling to the bottom if you try this road,' Sara said quickly. 'Are you staying here long?'

'Rest of the day,' Millicent Greenberg said with a grin at her husband. 'We'll get out before nightfall. I don't like travelling at night here.'

'And that's saying something!' her husband said proudly. 'Nothing and nobody scares Millie!'

Sara could think of somebody who would.

'Do you think you could...' she began hurriedly, but Millicent Greenberg interrupted with a gasp of admiration.

'Will you look at that, Eddie?' she said in an awe-stricken tone. 'I don't think I've ever seen anybody as marvellous-looking! Do you think he's one of those Mexican film stars?'

Sara's heart began to race, and she was quite prepared for the hand that came like a steel trap to her arm.

'We must go, Sara!' Jaime said softly, with a carefully hidden threat in his velvety voice. He nodded politely at the Americans, turning to lead her away at once, and she knew that the marks of his fingers on her arm would take a long time to fade.

'You had thought of escape?' he said in a grating voice as he slid her into the Land Rover and started the engine.

The last thing she wanted to do was give that fact away.

'I was simply having a friendly conversation!' she said huffily. 'Americans are very friendly people.'

He ignored that. Apparently he could see very easily through her deception.

'They are lucky that you did not beg for help. Had I come out and found you gone, it would not have taken much questioning to find out where and with whom!'

'And of course you would have raced after them and held them up on the road like a—a *bandido*!' she said heatedly, remembering his ready acknowledgement of her assessment of him.

'I do not need to perform such actions myself!' he growled angrily. 'One telephone call and they would have been stopped at the next place they came to! Their camper would not have been seen in Mexico again either, because permission to travel here would have been withdrawn permanently!'

'They're American citizens!' Sara said with a certain amount of violence, her bright idea beginning to fade away.

'And I am Carreras!' he said with devastating finality. It silenced her completely, and she sat with her head bowed as the Land Rover crawled steadily down the track they had so recently climbed.

She looked up in surprise when he suddenly pulled into a small clearing at the side of the track and switched off the engine, turning to her with a heavy sigh.

'The doctor says that you are fit,' he told her in a sombre voice. 'Everything is healed nicely.' He looked at her moodily, his dark eyes skimming her face. 'You are intent upon leaving? You are still fretting to get back to England?'

'You—you know I am!' she said in surprise. 'I—I've never wanted to be in Mexico!'

'And yet you came, risking your life in the process,' he reminded her, his vibrant gaze holding her own.

'Only to find my father, only to...'

'I want you to stay!' he said in an intense voice. 'I am tired of this game of pretending. Very soon I must get back to work. I cannot go on for much longer, ignoring the fact that I have responsibilities and that daily the telephone is ringing with people seemingly on the edge of hysteria, demanding my appearance. I want to be able to fly out to do what I must do, and go with the knowledge that you will be here when I get back!'

'It's no use threatening me!' Sara said in a whisper, unable to really believe the tone he was using.

'I am not threatening, Sara. This time I am asking, I am asking you to stay. I cannot simply let you go. I have known that for some time. If you had not flown out here, I would have come back to England and found you the moment that I could shake off my duties.'

'You couldn't possibly! You—you know what I am...I...'

'I want you!' he said vibrantly. 'I need you as the sun needs the sky. It is beginning to take up the whole of my mind, the whole of my dreams. I cannot face the idea of you being back in the arms of this man in England!'

Without warning he pulled her to him, his eyes searching her face as she looked up at him with wide blue eyes.

'I spend my days watching that you are safe, that you are well, spend my nights wanting you in my arms. Do you expect me to simply let you go, to hand you over tamely to someone else?'

'You—your life is planned,' she said in a tremulous whisper, knowing exactly what she was hearing, exactly what he meant.

'My life is planning itself,' he said passionately. 'It is planning itself around you, and there is nothing that I can do about it.' He pulled her towards him. 'Stay with me, Sara! I have never told a woman before that I needed her!'

Her eyes must have held some longing, because he groaned deeply and covered her mouth with his, his lips urgent but stingingly sweet. And she was lost again, as she was always lost close to him, drugged by his kisses, swept into enchantment. There was no resistance in her, not when he was holding her so tenderly, kissing her with a murmured plea deep in his throat.

Her arms came round his neck, her fingers burying themselves in his black hair, and he came to vibrant life, forcing her back against the seat, his body half over hers, his breathing heavy and harsh.

'*Dios*, little witch!' he muttered. 'You have picked a rare place to surrender to me. Were we in the house, you would by now be in my bed where you belong. This is only sharpening my hunger!'

He could not let her go, though, and she clung to him too as his lips trailed with fire over her cheeks and neck.

'I do not intend to let you go!' he breathed against her lips, and her sudden feeling of alarm was swamped by his hungry kisses, by the hands that swept over her possessively. When his hand slid into the neckline of her dress to search eagerly for her breast, she moved to accommodate him, wanting what he wanted. Memory and anger a thing of the past, her mouth opened beneath his as he plundered her sweetness, his caressing hand filling her with mindless pleasure.

'There is a limit to my endurance!' he said thickly after what might have been a moment or a lifetime—Sara was so lost in rapture that she had no thought of time or the world. 'We must go.' He cupped her hot face in his hands, hard and possessive, sure of her. 'You will not leave me! I will not let you go!' he said harshly. 'Without you in my arms I am bereft, hungry. It is over four months since I first kissed you, and I cannot touch any other woman! You are the one I want, the one I will have!'

He started the engine and pulled on to the track, the vehicle returning to the careful descent as Sara's thoughts made some attempt to adjust to this. He could not touch

María-Teresa, that was true. She was a high-bred Mexican with a dragon-like mother to guard her; in any case, she was to be his wife. His words, too, had sounded alarm bells in Sara's mind, alarm bells that rang above the weakness she felt after his caresses. Over four months! Her mind flashed back to William's words as he read out the copy of the will. 'If he should still be missing six months from the dating of this letter...' She had little time left in which to find her father. It was desperate!

'Jaime,' she said huskily, 'will you take me to find my father?'

'No!' he almost roared the word. 'I will give you anything and everything you need! Your search for wealth is finished! I am a millionaire many times over, and from now on we will live without any thought of your hunger for money entering our lives. The only hunger you need is the one I have for you!'

With the thought of her greed and lack of scruples always there before him, and a wife to share his life, she thought bitterly. Desperation flooded through her and she turned her head sideways, hiding away, not wanting to see the disgust that she knew would be on his face, not wanting him to see the determination that was on hers. She had never been a mistress to anyone, and she did not intend to start now. What she *did* intend to do was to get to her father and get out of here. The telephone at the house began to seem like the only way, unless a miracle happened.

The Mercedes was parked where Jaime wanted to park when they got back. Evidently someone had been about to use it, because it blocked their way at the front of the house, its nose turned to the gates, ready to leave.

He got out without a word, leaving her there, striding round the back, no doubt to find the culprit, and bitterness flooded through Sara. He had forgotten his tenderness as soon as she had mentioned her father, forgotten her too in his annoyance at this small thing. She sat where he had left her, her mind turning things over frantically. She was trapped! The days were speeding by and she would be left with the inheritance, her vow broken! Only the British Embassy could help her. Maybe they would send someone out?

She suddenly found her gaze intently on the Mercedes. Perhaps a miracle had presented itself, after all! The Americans would be there until later. They were kindly people, they spoke her language. Even if they would not risk taking her, they could get word to the Embassy.

She saw the mountain roads in her mind, the twisting bends, but the road to the village was not as bad as the road to town. The light was still good and she had been driving for years. With care, she could do it.

She got out and looked around. There was not a soul in sight. She ran to the Mercedes and breathed a sigh of relief. The keys were there. It was now or never.

The drive sloped away from the house, and as she released the handbrake the heavy car began to roll slowly and silently away, her stealthy departure unnoticed. It was not until she was within sight of the gate that she had need to start the engine.

They were just closing the gate and looked at her in surprise, but she copied Jaime's imperious attitude and waved her arm regally at them, her heart easing from its pounding as the gates swung back wide and she was free! For the first time in ages, she felt a weight lift from her mind, and she turned to the mountain road with a smile on her lips. Top that, Señor Carreras!

At first the road was not difficult, but there was a rather alarming drop to this part of the road. After this she knew that it twisted into the sharp rises that lead towards the village, no possibility of falling to the valley, but a stiff climb that was hard even for the Land Rover. She felt a momentary panic as she remembered belatedly that Jaime had said it was impossible to negotiate the road in anything other than a four-wheel-drive vehicle. The Mercedes was not that! Still, she was desperate. If she could get only part-way up, then she would walk the rest of the way; it had not been too far. Even now, though, she dared not go fast.

She heard the sound of the Land Rover even above the sound of the engine of the car, but she dared not take her eyes off the road, not even to look in the driving mirror. It had to be Jaime. He had found out. Nothing would make her stop though, and he couldn't pass.

He sounded the horn, a continuous blare of angry noise, but Sara ignored it, her legs trembling on the controls, her hands tightening on the wheel until they were white. She could imagine his face, his fury, and she bit into her lip until she felt actual pain.

There was a sudden roar of noise, an upsurge of dust on the rocky, mountain road, and the Land Rover passed her. The scream that rose in her throat was not from fear for herself, however. Drawn from the road by sheer terror for him, her eyes were glued to the far-side wheels of the Land Rover as they spun on the very edge of the drop to the valley. He had risked his life to stop her! She braked and put her head down on the steering wheel, tears pouring down her face as her mind imagined the Land Rover rolling down and down, Jaime falling to his death.

She was still like that when he came back, wrenching the door open and speaking in a voice she could hardly recognise.

'Get out! Get out and stand against the rock face!'

She had nothing on her mind but obedience, and she could not even look up as he got in and, to her horror, actually began to reverse. He went to a wider part of the road and parked tightly in, walking back, passing her without a glance to get into the Land Rover and reverse towards her.

'In!' He stopped by her and she opened the door and climbed in, her eyes fearfully on the drop, her mind unable to imagine how he had passed her at all. And she could not, dared not speak. He had to reverse almost to the gates of the estate and he said not one word, even when they were once more in front of the house. Instead, he dropped her and drove to the gates, and she knew that he was going back for the car, that it was a danger in its present position. Sara fled to her room, not even thinking about the outcome of her folly. Retribution would come, she was sure of that!

There not long to wait. Conchita came to her room, her face worried when Sara called for her to enter.

'Señor Carreras would like to see you, *señorita*,' she said quietly, and the fact that he was now no longer Señor Jaime to this spirited little woman was enough to tell Sara of his wrath.

Jaime was in his study, and Sara's heart sank further at the sight of his cold face. She simply stood there, waiting for the axe to fall, and he frowned impatiently, standing and coming to the door.

'Come in!' he said abruptly, indicating that she should precede him. 'We will not require any onlookers!'

'I want to leave! I want to leave as quickly as possible!' Sara said as the door of the study shut behind them. She could not afford any more delays. She felt well enough to travel and well enough to make a considerable fuss if he refused to let her go. She could not face this icy reserve, even though she knew she had deserved it.

'I can well understand that,' he grated. 'You are so anxious to leave that you were well prepared to steal my car and risk the mountain roads. You had made arrangements to meet the Americans?'

'No!' She had no intention of getting anyone else into trouble; she had troubles enough without also suffering the pangs of guilt. 'I intended to get them to contact the British Embassy. I'm still here only because I have no papers, no passport. Otherwise, I would have appealed to Señora Carreras. When I get to the British authorities, I'll be all right.'

'You are all right now, *señorita*,' he said coldly, walking to his desk. 'I have all the documentation that you need. While you were still in hospital I arranged that. They have been in my possession for several days.'

'You let me believe... You had them here all the time?' Sara felt furious, and it showed all over her face. 'Why didn't you tell me?'

'You were not fit to travel, and I know of your obsession,' he remarked coolly, leaning against his desk, the documents tossed carelessly on the desk top. 'I also wanted you to stay. I hoped that I could persuade you, but I can see that whatever you say, however you react to me, I will never be able to let you out of my sight. You were prepared to risk death, driving a car you do not know on mountain roads that you are ill-equipped to cope with. The Mercedes would not have held on the road to the village. Why do you imagine that I did not take it myself? You probably thought that I deliberately took you in a vehicle to shake you up? I did not! Any further and you risked an accident. You have made your point, *señorita*. In making you a prisoner, I make a prisoner of myself also. You may pick up your papers and go. I will arrange a flight for you to London at once!'

She had wanted this so much, but now that he was letting her go, dismissing her coldly, the only thing that was uppermost in her mind was the thought that she would never see him again. For seconds, she just stood there looking at him, blankly, trying to imagine what it would be like to look up and never see him.

If she told him the truth now, would he believe her? His hard words in London came back to her. He had not listened then, so why should he listen now? The magic of his arms would have to be forgotten. And there was María-Teresa, after all.

'I—I'm not going to England, *señor*. I came here to seek my father. There are now few weeks left before the time is up. I intend to start right away to look for him. When I get to Mexico City, I can begin again.'

She spoke quickly before her small courage could desert her, and there was a frightening silence that was broken as his face flared with fury.

'So! You are determined to pursue this unexpected windfall? Any papers that you had for your father to sign were lost in the fire after the crash. It is therefore pointless now to continue!'

'All I have to do is find him,' she said stubbornly, taking her cue from him as to attitude. He thought that she was a grasping and greedy female, it was written all over his face. Then let him think that! She swallowed the tears that threatened to come and tightened her lips.

'I've been thinking about that, and providing that I can find him and take back some proof that he's here, then the solicitors and the banks can cope with the rest. It will be up to them. Certainly, they'll not dare to hand the legacy on to the next person while my father is alive. He could sue them!'

'Or you could!' he said in a hard voice.

'Oh, I don't think that I'm going to need to, Señor Carreras. In any case, I'm not leaving Mexico until I find my father,' she said quietly.

'So! Let us get this straight!' he said bitingly, standing to walk to the window and gaze angrily out at the garden. 'You intend to fly to Mexico City, seek aid from your Embassy and then return to this part of the country in a ramshackle plane such as the one you hired to get here in the first place? The pilots of these planes often fly by sheer instinct and nothing more. They often have little instrumentation, and even if they have, few of them can understand it. Fog comes in the mountains quickly and unexpectedly. You are looking for another spell in hospital, Señorita Lawrence?' His voice had risen angrily, and he turned round to glare at her.

She was pale and trembling, his hard words reminding her of her fear when the plane crashed; but she had a promise to keep, a solemn vow that she had not undertaken lightly. She was not about to shrug that vow away because she feared flying into another fog.

'You don't understand,' she said with an edge of pleading. 'The money doesn't mean to me what you obviously think that it does. There's much more to it than that, I...'

'I really do not wish to know, *señorita*,' he interrupted harshly. 'Do not forget that I, too, have a memory. I know just exactly what lengths you are prepared to go to to get to your father. Are you now telling me that he means something to you?'

'No!' she snapped. He did not mean anything to her, she could only just remember him, but she could remember very well the misery he had left behind him. 'He means absolutely nothing to me! There is only one person in the world that I care about, and I can't get out of Mexico fast enough! However, I intend to get to my father and see to it that he claims the money from the legacy. No amount of arguing will stop me! If you will not get me back to Mexico City, then at least let me telephone my Embassy there, and seek help!'

'Oh, I will do better than that, *señorita*,' he said slowly, his eyes narrowing angrily when she spoke of her desire to leave Mexico. 'To go where you are intending, you need the best. I am the best, as I told you in London. There is no need to get in touch with your Embassy, or waste this valuable time in travel. As you are determined, I will take you.'

'But why?' She stood and faced him, her eyes filled with surprise that bordered on shock.

'Perhaps I do not wish to go through all the trauma of having you here after another crash, or after some imbecilic guide has taken a fancy to you and dragged you off into the mountains. You could easily become as lost as your father, and I cannot say that I find your judgement reliable. You would undoubtedly pick any rogue who presented himself.'

'The Embassy will...' she began, but he cut across her speech with a quiet savagery.

'Spare me the details of your imagination, *señorita*,' he rasped. 'The Embassy would put you on a flight for London and get you off their hands with great rapidity. I am dealing with people like that every time I come out of the mountains and find myself locked into the business of my own inheritance. I know their ways. If you intend to go to find your father, there is only one way that you are going to get there, and that is if I take you.' He glanced at her with dark and glittering eyes. 'Do not worry, *señorita*. I will not need payment. I will count the times that you have been in my arms as payment enough. The least I can do is see to it that you find your father!'

'Then I accept your offer of help, *señor*!' The constant harshness of his voice made her own temper rise over her misery. 'However, I need physical help only. I do not need advice or lectures!'

'Oh, I can quite see that,' he said scornfully. 'I realise that you have got it all thought out carefully. I expected nothing less of you.'

'Then you're not disappointed,' she said quietly. 'I would hate it, if having made up your mind about me from such a short time, you suddenly found that you had been wrong. It would be a great blow to your ego!'

He looked as if he would like to punish her for that remark, but before he could speak she looked away and turned to the door. Suddenly she was very weary, all the joy had gone out of her, and she remembered oh, so very clearly how it was when he had held her, how she would miss this unkind and arrogant man.

'I never thanked you for all that you've done for me,' she said in a low voice. 'Whatever you think of me, I want you to know that I will remember your help when I needed it so badly. I'm sorry too about my dangerous trick today. I never meant you to risk your life, and I know that you did.'

She began to walk from the room, but his voice stopped her, a little less harsh now. 'Sometimes, *señorita*, I count my life very cheap.'

'I—I don't really think that it is,' she said quietly. 'I'll wait for you to decide what to do, and then perhaps you could let me know.' She walked out and he did not try to stop her.

CHAPTER EIGHT

WITH a speed that assured her that he could not wait to get her out of the house, Jaime made all the necessary arrangements, calling her down to his study just before dinner.

'There are one or two things that I need to know before we embark on this expedition,' he said with an impersonal air that hurt, even though she had expected it. 'Firstly, do you ride a horse and do you ride well?'

'Yes to both questions,' she said quietly. Her grandmother had seen to that. It had been another chance to humiliate her mother, although Sara herself had been too young to realise it at the time.

'Well, we can only take the four-wheel-drive vehicle so far,' he told her. 'After that it is horseback all the way. And the way is rough,' he added with a look at her from beneath dark brows. 'You will need to wear tough clothes and boots. I have ordered them already, and they will be delivered early in the morning. After that, we will be able to leave. For myself, I am usually ready to leave at short notice, so it is nothing for Conchita to prepare the things that I need.' He glanced at her and raised his eyebrows. 'Something is bothering you, *señorita*?'

'I—well, I just don't know how you were able to order the things I need to wear. I mean you never asked me about my size...'

'The things that I bought you when you were in hospital seemed to fit reasonably well,' he said drily. 'I had no help then, so I did not feel that I needed help now.'

Thinking of the lingerie, her face flushed and his smile was rather sour.

'There is nothing erotic in choosing riding boots, *señorita*,' he said scathingly. 'And as to the others, it was a necessity. I always cope with necessities.'

'I'm sorry, Señor Carreras,' she said quietly. 'You won't have to cope with me again.'

'We will see. Meanwhile, come and look here.' He had a map spread out on the table, and she came forward to lean over and look closely at it. 'To the best of my knowledge, your father is here, in this area. You see the sort of terrain?'

She did. It could be summed up in one word—mountainous. His brown finger stabbed at the map.

'We are here. To get to your father we have no alternative but to go up into the mountains. Beyond is a plateau and there we will find him, if we are going to find him at all. You will need to travel light; it is not particularly easy, not even for a horse. Hot in the day and cold at night. I will attend to everything except your personal possessions. You are responsible for your own toiletries and clothes. Beyond that, nothing.'

'If I could help...' she began, but he folded the map deliberately and turned away.

'There is nothing that you can do for me, *señorita*,' he said coldly, and that just about summed up the situation. He had shut her out as she had imagined he would, and she turned to the door, trying to tell herself that it did not matter in the slightest.

* * *

By breakfast time next day, Jaime was ready to leave
and she was called to his study to find a pile of clothes
on a chair, low riding boots standing on the floor beside
them.

'Try these on and I will come to see them,' he ordered
coolly. 'I wish to know that they fit. If they do not, we
will postpone the trip until tomorrow.'

She simply picked them up and left the room. They
had nothing to say to each other, and she bit her lip in
anxiety when she wondered how they were going to
manage to be together on the trip without constantly
fighting.

The clothes were, as he had said, tough. There were
trousers in a sort of khaki twill, and a matching shirt
with long sleeves. She put them on and they were a
perfect fit, the boots short enough to make it possible
to tuck the trousers into them.

'Well?' He entered her room after the most brief tap
on the door, and she swung round to look at him in
exasperation, feeling foolish, like a child who was being
taken out and checked off for perfection first.

'They fit very well,' she said a little sharply. 'I'm ready
to go.'

'I will decide if they fit!' he grated, coming in and
bending to take her foot in his hand and examine the
boot's spare room around her slender foot. A grunt of
sound was all that she received as a comment on his
decision, and she was stunned and not a little outraged
when he stood and grasped the waistband of her trousers,
tugging it deliberately.

'Do not be alarmed, *señorita*,' he said with a smile
that contained no warmth. 'I wish to make sure that you
are going to be able to complete the journey. Tight

clothes and tight boots may look very nice, but they do not make for comfort.'

'I'm not bothered about comfort!' she snapped, pink-faced. 'I just want to get this over with.'

'I was not thinking of your comfort so much as my own,' he murmured sardonically. 'I will be the one at the receiving end of your grumbles, and if you are too distressed to continue, it will be my job to bring you back, and no doubt start the whole thing over again.'

He walked out before she could reply, pausing in the doorway to say briskly, 'They are a good fit. Now take them off and pack them. You will be travelling a great deal more comfortably today. Travel in a dress, or at the very least, something light. Do not forget sweaters for the cool of the evening. Downstairs I have a jacket for you. You will need it in the mountains. I will carry it.' She opened her mouth to speak, but he was gone, and she found irritation rising inside at his arrogance and his careless manner with her.

He was, however, an organised man. After lunch, as they set out in the sturdy Land Rover, she noticed the neat rolls of bedding, the complete absence of any kind of fuss that surrounded their possessions. He had shown her how to roll her things into a waterproof sheet and tie it securely, and she rather thought that this was the only instruction that she was likely to get.

The whole of the household had assembled to see them off, but he did not linger for even a moment. He simply flung up his arm in farewell and drove off, only María-Teresa receiving a smile from his hard, firm lips. And Sara was back where she had started, alone with a stranger, because his attitude had been that of nothing more than a guide.

He had said that he was the best, and she had never doubted it, but she wondered miserably how she was going to manage to sit in silence for the whole of the journey there and back. Jaime seemed to be quite ready to sit unsmiling and silent for ever. He was quite accustomed to setting off like this entirely on his own, and she rather suspected that he was glad to be off into the mountains, but annoyed that he had company. Certainly, his desire for her was not at all evident and, without that, she was merely a nuisance and a responsibility.

'How long will we be able to travel like this?' she found enough courage to ask after a while. He had told her that they would be travelling comfortably to begin with, but she had not noticed much of that. The heavy vehicle took obstacles without any hesitation, and the effect of the jerking and bouncing was not helping her to be easy in either mind or body. Jaime seemed impervious to any discomfort.

'There is a small *raneho* in the foothills about twenty miles away,' he informed her. 'As we were so late setting off, we will stay there tonight. I keep horses there and we can also leave the Land Rover. We will get an early start tomorrow.'

'How—how far altogether?' she asked, clinging to the side of the vehicle as he swerved skilfully around a huge rock with no slackening of speed.

'With any luck, two days out and two days back, not counting the *rancho*. You are tired of the trip already, *señorita*?'

Sara decided that it would be better not to answer. In fact, it would be better not to speak at all. She sat in silence, the hot sun beating down on her, burning her head, adding to her growing discomfort. Jaime seemed to be immune to it. He was wearing the things he had been wearing when she had seen him in the forest, his brown arms strong and sure across the wheel. She looked hastily away. It was better not to think of those arms and the way they felt when they were around her.

He reached into the back, and without warning slammed a hat on her head, a stiff white *sombrero* that she had seen the men on his property wear.

'Another thing that I bought you,' he said mockingly. 'It is a useful thing to possess. Not used, as most Europeans imagine, to sleep beneath, but to keep off the heat of the sun. Wear it all the time. You are not used to the ferocity of our sunshine, and I rather suspect that you will have troubles enough without sunstroke.'

He was, of course, quite right, and she fixed it more comfortably, trying then to close her eyes and sleep, a useless project. The thought of getting away from this bone-shaking form of travel and on to a horse was like the pot of gold at the end of a rainbow. However, she kept that thought to herself.

They came upon the *rancho* unexpectedly in the late afternoon. Rounding a bend in the rough, uneven track, they were suddenly faced with a level stretch of land that seemed to appear out of nowhere. The small house was surrounded by corrals, and a high building that was clearly a barn stood at the side.

It was a welcome sight, especially as one corral held horses and the prospect of mounting one and riding at her own speed lifted Sara's flagging spirits. When the Land Rover stopped, she had to make a great effort to move her legs to get out. She was stiff all over.

'Señor Carreras! *Bienvenido!*' A small Mexican with the thickest moustache that Sara had ever seen appeared from the house, followed by a plump wife and several children, and Jaime's face lit up with laughter.

'*Gracias, mi amigo! Qué tal estás?*'

He was at home here, as comfortable as he was at his own splendid house or in the luxurious suite of an hotel in London, and instantly he was surrounded by the children, all speaking at once.

He motioned Sara forward when they had been called to order by the smiling, plump little woman who looked shyly at Sara and blushed roundly at Jaime's greeting of her.

'They do not speak English,' he explained to Sara, 'but they want you to know that you are welcome.'

'Thank you.' Sara smiled at all of them, and there was an instant conference that had the small woman nodding vigorously.

'You are beautiful,' Jaime explained. 'They are all agreed on the fact. Juanita endorses the opinion.'

'Oh, *gracias*!' Sara now blushed in her turn, and there was delighted clapping of hands.

'Well done,' Jaime said softly. 'You have pleased them very much. Now they will be all over you to teach you the language. First though, I wish you to look at the horses with Diego and I, then you may rest.'

He led her to the corral, and she was glad to lean against the fence and watch the horses milling around, their coats gleaming in the sun. They were in beautiful condition, and at her remark about this, Jaime looked at her askance.

'Naturally,' he said with raised eyebrows. 'If a Mexican does not know horses, who does? Even our girls teach the *gringos* to ride.'

Chastened, she kept silent and stood in a truly docile manner while Jaime and Diego murmured together over the most suitable horse for her to ride.

'I ride well!' she finally muttered through clenched teeth. 'Just wheel one out!'

'This is Ronaldo,' Jaime said with a derisive look at her annoyed face as a huge bay moved against him, nuzzling his hand. 'He is mine. I keep him here all the time, and I know his abilities as I know my own. He will get me safely to wherever I wish to go, and it is not my riding skills that prevent him from tossing me over the edge of a precipice, it is his temperament! We are choosing a horse that is rock-steady in all circumstances, and you will see the circumstances the day after tomorrow. Have patience, and Diego will present you with a horse that may even save your life.'

'I'm sorry,' Sara's face was red, not only because of the sun. Jaime snorted in irritation.

'*Bueno*! I am trying to make sure that you have no cause for sorrow later!'

Silence and patience seemed to be advisable, and finally a grey with gentle eyes and a calm air about her was chosen.

'Pepita!' Jaime announced. 'After dinner you may get acquainted with her, and if she likes you, perhaps she will condescend to carry you into the mountains.'

'We are in the mountains!' Sara pointed out irritably, feeling tired and bad-tempered, but he took her arm with a wicked smile and pointed upwards.

'The Sierra Madre,' he said in a softly menacing voice. 'Your father is beyond the mountains. That is your destination, *señorita*!'

Sara looked up, her gaze following his outstretched arm, and her heart sank. The mists that had hovered all

day had miraculously cleared, and in the near distance,
rising ever upwards in magnificent grandeur, were the
mountains she had seen from her bedroom window. The
impassable barrier that barred her route to her father.
From the house they had been merely things of beauty,
distant and unattainable. Now they were here, above her,
disdainful of human effort. She stared, spellbound, awe
clearly on her face, and Jaime whispered tauntingly in
her ear.

'Now you see why you needed the very best guide,
señorita. Without me, you are incapable of reaching your
father. Remember *that* when your little temper surfaces.
If I decide to abandon you, you will never come back
to civilisation!'

She looked at him in momentary horror, but his mouth
was twisted in amusement, and she went off gladly when
Juanita indicated that she could wash at the house and
then get ready to eat.

In the morning, Sara awoke to find Jaime bending over
her, shaking her gently, his dark face enigmatic.

'I have brought you some warm water for your wash,'
he told her. 'Get up at once, and then we can start while
it is still cool.'

She nodded and made to get up straight away, only
realising belatedly that she was not dressed. She was still
in her silky nightdress.

'You travel in style, *señorita*,' he observed sardonically. 'Were Juanita to see you now she would be filled
with admiration.' He walked off when she simply glared
at him, but she looked round carefully before making
any further attempt to get up.

They had slept in the barn. Diego had offered to give up his bed for Sara, but she would not hear of it, and Jaime had approved of her resistance to the plan.

'It is not a good idea to separate a man from his wife,' he had remarked wryly. 'That is how friendships are lost.' So it had been the barn, and he had placed their bedrolls in the sweet-smelling hay, well separated from each other.

After a bad beginning, Sara had had the best night's sleep that she could remember, only one small incident marring it. As she had been drifting thankfully into sleep, a rustling had brought her to startled and uneasy attention, making her sit up nervously, afraid to ask Jaime what it was. He had told her, however.

'It is the horses, *señorita*. There is no cause for alarm. Two of them are in a stall at the far end of the barn. You may sleep in safety.' There had been derisive laughter in his voice when he'd added softly. 'Realise how fortunate you are. If you had come with anyone else, the sound that startled you might well have been the stealthy approach of your guide as he made his way to your bed.'

There was no suitable reply to that and Sara had kept silent, settling down again and curling into her blankets.

'You are very trusting, *señorita*,' he'd observed quietly. 'You are prepared to sleep with me so close?'

'I can scream very loudly!' she had felt driven to reply, and his next words had made sure that she would go to sleep with a flush on her cheeks.

'I have never noticed that so far, *señorita*!'

Now, with the barn to herself, she hastily washed, thankful of the warm water because it was very chilly as yet. When she went outside, she saw that the mists of the morning had not yet cleared. The sun was still behind the mountains and the mists hung in wreaths around the yard and few scattered trees.

She was glad of the heavy jacket that Jaime tossed to her from the Land Rover when they were preparing to leave after a light breakfast, and the idea of a long-sleeved shirt did not now seem so foolish. She gathered her belongings and rolled them carefully into her pack, watching intently as Jaime fastened her bedroll and this personal pack to the back of the saddle of her horse. This was probably the only time that he would demonstrate the manoeuvre, and she could well do without his sarcastic comments.

'I've not packed the dress that I wore yesterday,' Sara mentioned as casually as she could. 'I won't be needing it in the mountains, and I wondered about giving it to Juanita, if you don't mind. She was so filled with admiration for it last night when we had our meal that I hate to simply leave it and then collect it later. I'm sure she'll be drooling over it while we're away. I know that I would. As I won't be taking anything back to England, it would be a reward for her kindness.'

'It is your dress, *señorita*,' he said, giving her a sour look. 'You may do with it as you wish. However, I rather think that Juanita will have some trouble getting into it.' He glanced at Juanita as she stood in the doorway, watching their preparations for departure with an interested smile on her face. 'She is built on rather more substantial lines than you. If you wish to please her,' he added testily, 'I can buy a similar one in a larger size and send it to her in your name when you have returned to England.'

His casual acceptance of her going, and his apparent skill in buying female garments, had her turning away abruptly.

'Thank you, I would like that very much. I can see that you're quite accustomed to buying dresses and other things for your female companions, so maybe it won't be too much of an imposition. Of course, I'll send you the money.'

She was speaking thoughtlessly again, jealousy tearing through her at the idea of Jaime's arms around any other woman, and his reaction was no less angry.

'I do have female companions when the mood takes me, *señorita*,' he snapped, 'but I am not accustomed to providing them with clothes! You are the only woman that I have—*kept*!'

He tossed her the reins of Pepita and swung into the saddle of his own horse with a lithe grace that spoke of natural horsemanship. 'Mount up!' he ordered sharply. 'We are ready in good time and I would like to get away now. The sooner we start, the sooner we will be back here and the whole affair ended!'

Sara too swung up into the saddle of Pepita, aware all the time of the hard, black gaze on her. If now she had been incapable of riding, he would probably have dismounted and beaten her. She vowed to hold her tongue in future, and bit hard on her lip when the thought of someone in Jaime's arms flashed across her mind again. It was something that she would have to forget, just as she would have forget him and this time in Mexico.

By noon, they had climbed high into the mountains, the trails rough but by no means dangerous, the horses surefootedly picking their way upwards. At first she had enjoyed it to the point of exhilaration, following Jaime as he picked out the trails, sitting easily on the great bay, Ronaldo. By the time they called a halt for food however, Sara was exhausted, aching all over. This was no canter across an English meadow; the climb was steep and the movement of the horse was bruising. It was years since she had ridden, but she had not mentioned that to Jaime, afraid that he would refuse to bring her.

Already deep into the Sierra Madre, the trail that they had followed in the Land Rover miles away, looking like a faint dusty ribbon far below, they rode through thick scrub and coarse grasses, tall and strangely shaped cactus appearing unexpectedly, and she was really very thankful when Jaime rode to the side of the track and dismounted under a few stunted trees.

'We will have our lunch,' he said coldly, his eyes on the distant peaks. 'There is a possibility that the air will cool in a while by the look of the sky over there. We will watch it as we eat, and then hope to continue in less tiring weather.'

It was not the weather—although the heat was now severe—it was the unaccustomed exercise that was taking its toll on Sara, and dismounting proved to be a problem. Her legs were stiff and unwieldy, and her spine felt bruised, among other things! She sat back in the saddle and was dismayed to find herself on the edge of tears. It had been utterly exhausting, and if Jaime snarled at her now, she would break down and cry.

She found herself being lifted from the saddle, his arm supporting her as her legs gave way.

'Just exactly how long is it since you rode a horse?' he asked irascibly when she was at last able to walk to the shade of the trees.

'A few years,' she confessed, avoiding his eyes. 'But I can ride!'

'Oh, yes!' he snapped. 'I can see that. However, you ride like a young lady in an English gymkhana! You are proposing to live in the saddle for four days at least, and unless I am to spend every night massaging your limbs you will have to change your style at once. Before we leave here you must learn to ride with the horse, not against her.' He moved away, leaving her subdued. 'Walk about for a few minutes while I prepare some food, and then you will recover. We have not come far, so little damage can have been done by now.'

Sara felt that they had come at least a hundred miles, and she could see little sympathy on his face, but she did exactly as he told her, walking gingerly up and down, relieved to find that at least some circulation came back into her legs and that her back was not now so painful.

She watched his capable brown hands as he prepared a light meal, watched the black shine of his hair as he bent to the small fire he had made, and a feeling of loneliness came flooding through her that kept her eyes on him with a tragic light in their deep blue depths.

To think of never seeing him again! To think that those strong brown hands would never reach for her, never touch her! He had been so right, her body knew its own needs, but it was much more than that and sadly she admitted it.

He was so many people: elegant and handsome in the London gathering, powerful and businesslike in his own affairs, tough and capable in the mountains. So many men in one tall, lean, handsome frame—and she loved them all.

'Collect your food, *señorita*,' he said sharply. 'The exercise will do you good!' He glanced up quickly, his gaze intensifying at the look he had surprised on her face, and when she simply looked away, her eyes clouding, he stood slowly and brought the plate over to her, holding it until she looked up.

'Things are not so very bad,' he said quietly. 'The time will pass quickly and soon all this will be forgotten. Eat your lunch,' he added with a rough edge to his voice. 'I will then give you a quick lesson in survival on horseback and we will be on our way.'

And that was exactly what he did, that and no more, making her ride in circles in the limited space, teaching her to go with the motion of the horse and relax in the saddle until finally, satisfied, he declared her ready to continue.

They spoke very little during the afternoon, steadily climbing higher into the *sierras* until the sun waned and the cool air began to bring a shiver to her skin. They seemed to be alone in the whole expanse of the mountains, and it was therefore with a feeling of being in a dream that Sara found that they were suddenly riding into a village.

Isolated, perched high in the *sierras* like an eagle on a crag, the Indian village was of reasonable size, its small central square surrounded by the adobe houses of the villagers and a small white church built off to the side. A white-robed priest came out to greet them as they waited, still mounted, surrounded by the Indians who obviously knew Jaime, but who watched Sara with black, interested eyes.

'Señor Carreras! *Bienvenido!*' The young priest strode forward and Jaime dismounted as he went to greet him, speaking English for Sara's benefit.

'We are going over the pass, Father Ovando. The English *señorita* is searching for her father, and we believe that he is in the region of the eastern valley. We would like to stay here overnight.'

'You are a welcome sight, Señor Carreras, and you are most welcome, *señorita.*' Father Ovando spoke quietly to the Indians in a tongue that was not Spanish as far as Sara could tell, and they laughed heartily, stepping back and away from Sara and the impassive Pepita. Her eyes anxiously sought Jaime, and to her surprise he smiled at her, coming then to lift her from her horse.

'What did he say?' she whispered, and he smiled even more widely.

'They have been admiring your hair,' he said with an amused look at her anxious face. 'Father Ovando pointed out to them that you were English, and that in England it is considered to be very ill-mannered to openly admire someone. They found that highly amusing, being an open and forthright people.'

'I—I thought they were—hostile,' Sara confided in a whisper. She found herself at the receiving end of another sardonic smile.

'They are, as I am, Mexican,' he said proudly. 'We are famous for our hospitality. We are never hostile!'

'You're more often than not hostile to me!' she said reproachfully, her eyes deeply blue in the gathering dusk as she looked up at him.

'You are in a category of your own!' he answered firmly, taking the reins of the two horses and leading them to the front of the church. 'Do not pick a quarrel with me at this moment, I beg of you, *señorita*. Father Ovando is a very pious man, and not accustomed to seeing a young lady spanked soundly. I realise that you are tired and not a little nervous, but do not make the mistake of taking your displeasure out on me!'

Due to the unmistakable gleam of annoyance in his dark eyes, Sara kept silent, and she found herself being taken care of with a very gentle solicitude as the priest led them to the small white hut that was built quite close to the church.

'This is our accommodation for travellers, *señorita*,' he said with an anxious look at her. 'Señor Carreras, of course, is quite used to sleeping here, but there is no separate accommodation for—er—ladies. There are two beds, though,' he added hopefully.

'It is luxury, Father!' Jaime asserted. 'Last night we slept in a barn, and the *señorita* was a little anxious about the rustling in the straw. She will be very comfortable here with her bedroll on a real bed. Of course, I can always sleep outside on the ground, but she is rather nervous when I am not within calling distance. We will manage very well.'

Honour satisfied, the young priest left them to bring in their possessions, after inviting them to eat with him in half an hour. Sara turned furiously on Jaime.

'How dare you tell him that I was frightened without you?' she stormed quietly, quite sure that all the villagers would be outside the windows listening.

'I spoke only the truth,' he said with a look of mocking astonishment on his face. 'You were uneasy even at Diego's house, and your remarks about the villagers here prove it!'

'Only because I realise that I'm quite helpless here without you!' she raged in a low voice. 'At least I could imagine that I'd be safe with you!'

'And now, you realise that I am a villian?' he asked with an impatient look.

'I...I... No! It's not that and you know it!'

'It is because you are anxious that Father Ovando does not get the wrong impression about us? Do not alarm yourself, *señorita*. He knows me well.'

She suddenly turned away, frustrated and tired, her limbs aching and her mind still unhappily acknowledging that she would find it very hard to live in a world where he was not there for her to see. If he did not leave her to recover in private, she would cry.

'Please leave me alone, Jaime,' she whispered, forgetting to be formal with so much more on her mind.

'That I cannot do,' he said softly.

He lifted her into his arms and held her quite still, looking into her eyes, and the peace that his arms brought spread through her aching body, making her head droop to his shoulder like a tired child.

'Why are we so angry?' she asked plaintively as he placed her on the bed, pulling off her boots and standing to look down at her with shuttered eyes.

'You are tired,' he said quietly, 'and we are frustrated. We want each other.'

'I—I don't! I don't want...'

'It is in your eyes, Sara,' he said softly, 'and it is in my mind and my body. It was in your eyes this afternoon when you looked at me. It is stupidity to deny the obvious. We wanted each other on sight, and it cannot be argued away. It is patterned into each of us like a life force.' He reached forward and smoothed her hair with a strong, brown hand, his touch gentle. 'Rest a while and I will see to the horses. Then we will freshen up and dine with Father Ovando.'

Sara's exhaustion came to her aid when she eventually managed to get herself ready for the simple meal that Father Ovando offered. She could hardly keep her eyes open, and this was so obvious that, for the most part, the conversation went completely over her head. She was not surprised when finally Jaime abandoned English and returned to his own language for the comfort of the priest.

She knew little else after that. She remembered getting out of her clothes and falling into the bed that Jaime had made up for her, and then, nothing, just blissful sleep until morning.

CHAPTER NINE

IT WAS colder. They were now high into the Sierra Madre, and Sara was glad to be on the move when they had eaten and were ready to leave. Once again, the warm water had been provided, and it had dawned on her that it was Jaime who was doing her this service. It was a kindness that did not really surprise her. When she thought back over things, he had been kind to her throughout her stay in his country. Only his words were harsh, his opinion of her the only real cruelty about him.

She watched him lead out the horses as she stood shivering by the small hut that had been their resting-place, and she counted the days to when she would never see him again. Two days out and two days back, not counting the *rancho*. The days were being used up quickly, and it was as if she was counting off the days to the end of life.

'I wish you luck, Señorita Lawrence.' The young priest was at her elbow as she looked round. She had been so busy watching Jaime as she stood huddled in the thick jacket, that she never noticed Father Ovando's approach. 'I have told Señor Carreras that it is some time since we have heard of your father, but then, that is not unusual. The Indians who have become his friends do not appreciate visitors, and they tend to protect him as one of their own. I hope that you will find him easily.'

'Thank you, Father. I hope so, too. Time is important.' He looked at her with a faint smile and she realised that, to him, time was not important at all. The

149

vow that she had made, though, was very different from his vows, and he did not have this heavy feeling inside that she had. It was astonishing to think that only to her would Jaime Carreras become unattainable. To this man he would always be available, whenever he was needed. She needed him, but he would soon be out of her life for ever. She was glad when they finally rode from the village, nobody to see their departure but the white-robed priest.

In spite of the altitude, the sun came out and established dominance. If anything, it was more hot than usual, and their progress was slowed by the increasing difficulty of the terrain. There were still tracks, but they were more suitable, Sara thought, to mountain goats than to riders. Today, Jaime was very silent, back to his attitude of sharpness, his cold looks, and she knew that she was the only one who had had a change of heart.

She had been too involved with her own feelings about Jaime to think deeply about what would happen when she reached her destination, but now, as she rode slowly behind him, the sun glaring down, so high now that they were actually looking down on mountains, she allowed her thoughts to wander where they had not been allowed to go before.

What would her father look like? How would she greet him? She had been brought up to think of him with bitterness, and it was not possible to banish that bitterness now. She blamed him as she had always blamed him for the hardships that her mother had suffered, for her mother's unhappiness and many small humiliations. He had lived his life as he had chosen, caring nothing for his responsibilities.

The thought brought memory with it, words that Jaime had said when he had first brought her from the hospital. 'It is the way I have chosen to live my life!' He, too, went into this wilderness, coming out when the mood took him. His wife, too, would be left alone and unhappy. The thought only served to increase her own bitterness and misery, although she would not be that wife left to wait alone.

She reined in, startled as one of her tightly rolled packages fell to the ground, rolling to the edge of the path and the scrub that grew there. It was her nightdress and spare shirt, and she muttered crossly, leaping down to get it. This morning she had been careless. Her hands had been cold and she had been too busy watching Jaime to attend to things properly. It served her right.

'Wait!' Her sharp request had Jaime turning round quickly in the saddle and he called to her urgently, but she was not really listening. Her mind was on other things, her eyes on the irritating roll of possessions that had been the cause of her dismounting. She ran across the track and reached for it, stumbling as she did so on legs that had suddenly been asked to take her weight, and then fear, stark and blinding, brought her sharply to reality.

The scrub was a thin veil covering a great drop, a drop that, in her moody and distant contemplation, she had not noticed. The land fell away without warning, and she was on the very edge of a plunge of hundreds of feet, visible from horseback if she had looked, deceptively screened from the sight of anyone on foot.

She swayed on the very edge, still not quite balanced, nauseated by the sudden sight of the yawning space, certain that she would fall, unable to help herself at all.

There was a flurry of sound and then she was hurled away from the danger, the impetus of Jaime's charge sending them both off their feet to fall back on to the hard path and roll over and over towards the horses, who stamped their protest but remained rock-steady.

'You incompetent little fool!' Jaime had landed on top of her, his arms lashed around her, protecting her from the rough path. His face was darkened with fury, and she could do nothing but stare back into his glittering eyes. 'If I get you out of these mountains alive, it will be a miracle!'

He stared at her for one burning second, and then his hard mouth swooped down on hers, hurtful and grinding, crushing her soft lips with only one thought, to punish. Tears started to her eyes at this savagery, but she made no move to resist, and when he lifted his head she lay there passively, her eyes tightly closed.

'Are you hurt?' His voice was rough-edged, and she opened her eyes to face his anger, but when he saw the tears that shone in the blue of her eyes, his face tightened with remorse. 'You drive me to the very limits of endurance, do you know that, English girl?'

Sara shook her head, unable to speak, noticing with an almost fatalistic detachment how her body had softened to meet his. Colour raced across his high cheekbones as possession flared in his black eyes, and his hand came up to cup her head, lifting it towards him.

'Kiss me, Sara!' he ordered harshly. 'Kiss me as I have so often kissed you!'

Her arms pulled free from his tight hold and wound around his neck, her fingers moving into the thick blackness of his hair, pulling his head to hers as her lips searched for his in a soft and pleading kiss. It would be the last time ever, the rest of her life only built on memories of this, and her mouth was soft and sweet, utterly giving.

His whole body seemed to be listening, waiting, poised on the edge of desire, and she moved against him, softly adjusting to the hard body that covered her own. It was a small movement, timid and gentle, but his reaction was instant and wild. He caught her to him more tightly, his body urgent as he took the initiative away from her and kissed her with a deepening passion.

'If we were anywhere but here, I would possess you now, and the devil take the consequences!' he muttered heatedly against her mouth. 'Do you believe me now when I tell you that we want each other? A moment ago, all I wanted to do was punish you for your stupidity, for giving me such a fright. The moment that I touch you, though, all thoughts but one leave my head!'

He wrapped her in his arms, his hands holding her face to his as he trailed kisses over her tender skin, tasting her lips with quick, hard movements of his mouth. For seconds, they strained together, their breathing harsh and uneven, then he got to his feet, pulling her up to stand in front of him as he looked down at her with self-mockery.

'Dust yourself off, *pobrecita*,' he said quietly. 'I am not about to set a record for the most uncomfortable place to make love.' He glanced across the path. 'Your package went over the edge. What did you lose?'

'My nightie and my spare shirt,' she said tremulously, unable to recover as he had done with such amazing speed.

'That is not important, then,' he said, his voice softly derisive. 'You will have to sleep as nature made you, as I do. Failing that, I have a spare shirt that I will not need. I do not carry nightwear, but I am always well equipped with spare shirts.'

Her blushes went unnoticed, however, because his eyes were suddenly riveted on the high peaks.

'Mount up quickly!' he said, with an urgency in his voice that gained her immediate attention.

He took her arm, hurrying her to the horses, the speed almost making her run.

'What is it?' His intensity alarmed her and he spoke without pausing.

'A storm, almost upon us. We do not have long to get to the next place, but we must. The going is too dangerous to be caught out in the open. Not far ahead there is an old hut. It is very primitive, and I had not intended us to stay there, but it is at least shelter both for us and the horses. We must get there before the storm breaks. At least, we must get off this particular track.'

He boosted her into the saddle, mounting his own horse at once, and Sara looked up to the towering peaks above them. Great clouds were moving over the highest peaks, black clouds that boiled angrily, and already in the far distance she could see sheets of rain that began to black out the blue of the sky. She needed no urging onwards.

They rode at last into a rocky clearing, a place that looked like a hideaway for bandits in some old film. An adobe hut nestled against the farthest rock face, a mean and dirty-looking place that would normally have horrified her. She was hardened now, though, to the mountains, looking with no surprise at the unexpected. The fast-approaching storm was more on her mind than any possibility of dirt.

Jaime led the horses to a lean-to at the side, and Sara moved to the door, carrying as many of their belongings as she could. It creaked on old hinges as she pushed, but Jaime's voice stopped her as she would have walked straight in.

'Wait!' He came round the side of the hut, the rest of their possessions with him. 'Let me go in and check the place out. It is some years since this place was occupied by anyone.'

Sara stood back and waited, her eyes returning to the gathering storm, glad when he came to the door and motioned her inside. It was dusty but it was dry, and there was an oil lamp, half-full.

'Generous of someone to leave that,' she observed into the silence.

'It is mine,' Jaime told her. 'I have been here before. Anyone following would not remove it. There is a code among travellers that is never broken.'

Not that there was much to steal anyway, Sara observed. There was a battered and scarred table, two rickety chairs, a rather grubby-looking bowl and an open, blackened fireplace.

'Home!' Sara breathed with a mocking sigh, and Jaime's dark eyes flashed to her in amusement.

'Believe me, you will be glad of shelter when the rain comes, and it is not too far away. We have our own cooking utensils, our bedrolls, food to eat. It is the Hilton at this moment.' She looked sceptical and he smiled to himself. 'Get the food out and I will try to get some fuel before the storm breaks.'

Even as he opened the door there was a driving wind that threatened worse to come, and Sara knelt by the packs, diving into Jaime's second pack for the food. Vegetables, tinned. Sweet potatoes, tinned. Meat, dried. It was nothing to get elated about. So far they had only needed midday meals, and Jaime had managed to produce things that were at least passable. She knew that tonight it was up to her, but the only thing that suggested itself was a stew. It was shattering to think how reliant she had become on Jaime. She searched for the can opener.

'Not cordon bleu, but decidedly edible!' Jaime pronounced later as they sat at the table, finishing the last of the stew. There was a state of truce between them, each trying to be perfectly normal in an unnatural situation. Outside there was turmoil. The storm had struck before dark, some kindly saint giving Jaime the time to make a fire and collect enough fuel to keep it going. The horses were sheltered but restless, and, as Sara's eyes met his and darted away for the twentieth time, Jaime signed resignedly and stood.

'I shall have to look at the horses. It would be a great misfortune if we were to awake tomorrow to find that they had pulled free and wandered.'

He left abruptly and Sara bit her lip anxiously. There was too much emotion in the air, neither of them in much doubt as to the other's feelings. She cleared the dishes, although there was no water in which to wash them. When Jaime came back she would ask him to put them outside—there was plenty of water there!

He didn't come back. It was impossible to know how long he had been, she had been too wrapped up in her own thoughts to notice things like that, but she knew that he was only at the side of the house. He should have been back long ago.

A few minutes more and she began to imagine every accident possible, until she ran to the door and forced it open against the driving rain.

'Jaime!' She called several times but there was no reply, and without thought she ran into the rain, reeling under the strength of it, making for the side of the hut, shouting at the top of her voice.

She screamed as two arms came tightly round her, only relaxing as Jaime yelled at her over the noise of the storm and forced her back to the open door of the hut, into the warmth of the firelit room as he slammed the door and fixed the bar in place.

'Is there something wrong with your mind?' he roared. 'Are you driven constantly to seek danger? We are in the mountains! I have told you about the dangers of going out at night! Why do you think I sought shelter for us so speedily?'

She stared at him angrily, furious with him for giving her such a fright.

'You were *ages*! How was I to know that you were safe? Look at me, I'm soaking!'

'I am not,' he said calmly, 'but then, I did not race outside in a panic. He was standing there in his long black cape, the water shining on it, his hair sleek and wet, black as the night. He looked devilish, smug and infuriating. Sara flew at him in a rage.

'I thought you were dead, you callous, hard-bitten...'

He caught her up, stopping her impetus by clasping her tightly to him and trapping her arms.

'Now you are more wet than ever,' he pointed out with irritating logic, his face relaxing into a smile at her wildly angry expression. 'I am not dead,' he assured her softly, his hands smoothing her dripping hair. 'Now seems a good time to get ready for bed. Hang your clothes on the back of the chairs and we will leave them in front of the fire tonight.'

He ignored her sulks and swung the cape free, hanging it behind the door and bending straight away to unroll the beds.

'Can I have a blanket to—to get changed behind?' Sara asked peevishly, towelling her hair and watching him in irritation.

'No!' he said evenly, carrying on as if she was merely childish. 'To make a bedroll like this is a work of art. I am not about to unmake them until we are back at the house and this expedition over.'

'But...'

'I am prepared to turn my back for a few seconds, however,' he interrupted smoothly. 'Make the most of it. The time has already started.'

His words shocked Sara into instant action, and she dealt swiftly with her wet clothes, keeping a wary eye on him all the while. It was only as she stood with his towel around her that she remembered the whereabouts of her nightie, at the bottom of the ravine!

'Can I borrow that shirt, please?' she asked with as much grace as possible, in case he said no, but he nodded uninterestedly and fished it out of his pack, staring at her in the firelight for a second as he handed it to her, his eyes sweeping over her. Then he turned away, just as her heart threatened to be heard over the storm.

Remembering his words, Sara closed her eyes tightly as he undressed. The lamp was out now, but the fire was blazing merrily, and she had long since stopped worrying if it would burn the hut down. It was oddly peaceful, even though the rain still lashed against the door and the thunder rolled threateningly over the mountains. She closed her eyes, beginning to drift off to sleep, until a new worry occurred to her.

'Jaime,' she said in a whisper, wondering if he was asleep. 'Jaime.'

'Yes?' He sounded wide awake and she was glad of that.

'Do you think that there's anything in here?'

'What exactly did you have in mind?' he asked mockingly, but she was too worried to be annoyed.

'Things like—like spiders, insects and...'

'Crawling, unspeakable monsters of minute size?' he finished for her with a low chuckle. 'Possibly. The rain is not acceptable to small, furry insects any more than it is to us, but I can assure you that there is nothing in here to harm you. I looked!'

'I'll never sleep now!' Sara exclaimed desperately, shooting up in bed and anxiously scanning the firelit floor. 'I'd rather face a mountain lion!'

'Definitely, you would not!' he assured her. He raised himself on one elbow. 'Get up!' he ordered.

'Why?' Her eyes were round and frightened, and he shook his head despairingly.

'Because I cannot, for reasons you can imagine. You are already shocked and frightened—I would not like to drive you over the edge! Come along!' he urged when she started at him with red cheeks, his meaning dawning on her slowly. 'I am not about to send you to stand outside the door like a naughty girl, although I now realise why I always travel alone.'

Sara got up carefully, her eyes still glancing around, and he reached out and pulled her bed close to his.

'There!' he said in a satisfied voice. 'They now have a choice. I assure you that they will choose me. Go to sleep!'

He closed his eyes and ignored her, and she got into her bedroll again, not one bit reassured. In fact, she was more frightened than ever. He was asleep so quickly, clearly used to this sort of thing, and she felt utterly alone. The fire sent dancing, moving shadows across the room that took on hideous shapes; every small sound was a spider of enormous size, and she lay stiff and scared until in desperation she put out her hand and touched Jaime's shoulder, needing contact with him to still her fright.

It worked, but it reminded her that soon she would never be able to touch him again, never see his face, and a low murmur of unhappiness escaped from her lips as tears swam in her eyes. She knew now what had happened to her as she had looked at him that first time. She knew why she had been unable to look away. Without any thought, her hand touched his hair, lingered and then moved away as she closed her eyes. He would never be for her.

Her hand was taken by strong fingers, and as she opened her eyes, startled and unhappy, he raised her palm to his lips, his dark eyes acknowledging her tears.

'You are tired, Sara,' he said softly. 'Do not invite that which you will regret tomorrow. You know I want you, and we are here in that hut in the mountains that you imagined. It is not an ideal setting and you are too vulnerable.'

He leaned over her and slowly kissed her lips, a smile on his face that was rueful and amused as he lifted his head.

'If you had been angry and waspish, I would have made love to you, do you know that, *señorita*?' His hand cupped her face almost tenderly. 'But you are afraid of the dark, worried about what you will find at the end of your journey. At this moment you are defenceless, and I am no savage. Go to sleep, *pequeña*. There is nothing to fear.'

Jaime lay back and she closed her eyes. She felt more close to him at this moment than she had ever felt, and she marvelled that he had not seen the longing in her eyes. Love for him blotted out every past thing, every harsh word, and she drifted into sleep with his hand still enclosing hers.

The pass was not as bad as she had dreaded. It was high and narrow, but no great problem for the horses. Jaime urged her to look straight ahead and leave any decisions to Pepita, and this was what she did because the drop to the side was horrendous. He, however, seemed to be completely at ease, and Ronaldo simply moved steadily along, his quiet rhythm giving her the confidence to continue. And it was, after all, for a very short spell only.

They rode out into the sunlight of the late afternoon quite suddenly and, nestling below them, in one of those hidden valleys so unexpected but so frequent in the mountains, was the village where she would find her father.

'If he is not here, then we are not going to find him this trip,' Jaime said, reining in Ronaldo and moving to ride beside her on the wider track. 'I do not know these Indians, and I very much doubt if they have even heard of me, so they may not be at all helpful. If he does not wish to be found here, you may be assured that we will not find him. We will not be allowed to find him.'

Sara merely nodded and looked down on the huts that were spaced around a clearing. Unlike the other villages she had seen in Mexico, including the one where Father Ovando had his mission, this one seemed utterly primitive.

What could it be about a man that he would abandon his wife and small child to their fate in order to live here, far from civilisation, far from those he had once professed to love? She would have nothing to say to him, would not be able to think of any topic of conversation, would not be able to answer if he should ask about her mother. She looked straight ahead and made no attempt to converse with Jaime, her deep silence and tightened lips bringing a quick frown to his face.

He said nothing however, and they descended to the valley floor, aware long before they reached the village that they were objects of curiosity to many eyes. By the time they rode into the clearing, it seemed that the whole of the population had turned out to look at them. Greetings, however, were noticeably missing.

With unerring instinct, Jaime picked out the headman and addressed him in a clipped and rather guttural tongue that Sara had never heard before. She knew that there were many Indian languages, and she wondered if Jaime knew them all. It would not have surprised her in the least. Jaime's quick speech, however, had a very startling effect. Suddenly she was the centre of all eyes; Jaime was ignored, and the old man who had watched Jaime with suspicion came to stand by Pepita, his hand on the bridle, his speech rapid and almost gentle.

'Jaime?' Sara turned helplessly to Jaime as he simply listened, never once intervening. He came towards her, dismounting and lifting her down from her horse to hold her steadily in front of him.

'He is telling you that you are welcome,' he said quietly. 'I am also welcome, as I come with you. Sara, your father is dead. He died four years ago, and he is buried here. I am sorry. All I can tell you is that they honoured him and they are worried that you have come to take him away, although they acknowledge your right.'

Dreadfully, she felt nothing. She was horrified by the fact, and she knew that Jaime and the watching Indians expected some show of emotion, some sign of grief. But

there was no grief; all of that had been used long ago—
grief for her mother and for the life they had led. This
man, buried somewhere here in an alien land, was not
able to bring one sorrow more to her, no tear to her eye.
She saw Jaime's intent narrow eyes, and she was grateful
for the interruption of the man who had spoken to her
at such length.

'He is offering to take you to the grave and to leave
you there to come to terms with your sorrow,' Jaime
said, his voice carefully controlling the derision that she
knew was there.

'Thank you. I would like that.' She conveyed her
thanks to the man with a small bow that he understood.
'Will you come with me?' She touched Jaime's arm,
finding it stiff and unyielding, his face, when she looked
up, aloof and cold.

'But of course. We will go at once and get it over
with. Your search is at an end. We cannot recross the
pass tonight, but we will leave at first light and get back
to civilisation as quickly as possible.'

He had nothing to say to her as they followed the old
man into the trees that clothed the valley floor, and
nobody made any attempt to come with them. There
was a waiting here, a silent acknowledgement that she
might well decide to claim her father and transport him
home. What would they think if they knew, as Jaime
knew, that her silence and her pale face were not a silence
or a pallor of grief, but of frustration, that even at the
very end her father had escaped his responsibilities and
made her vow impossible.

The grave was set apart from the others. Apart and
yet belonging. She was shocked to find that it was a
comfort to see that he was remembered with affection

and respect. Her mother's place of rest always looked cold, lonely, but somehow there was no loneliness here.

She stood for a few minutes, her eyes on the small area where her father rested, and then she turned away. Her search had ended, her reaction had confirmed to Jaime what he had always thought. She wanted to go home, home to her dearest William, her cousin and best friend. She needed to talk, and there was no one who would understand but William. She would go home at once.

'You can tell them I will not take my father home,' she told Jaime quietly. 'Tell them I am grateful that they cared for him and that he is buried here in the only place he wished to be, with the only people he cared about.'

He shot her an oblique, quizzical look, but he told them, waiting until they had once again reached the village, speaking so that they could all hear. There was an almost audible release of tension, a feeling that swept through them all and brought faint smiles to their rather forbidding faces.

'We are invited to stay the night, and we have little alternative,' Jaime informed her, looking at the darkening sky. 'Your father's small house is placed at our disposal. It is kept as it has always been, but as you are his daughter, you are welcome to use it.'

'No!' The words left her throat as soon as he had spoken, and he glanced at her with mounting annoyance.

'You are superstitious? You imagine that harm will befall you if you sleep in the house where he slept?' His sharp comment angered and hurt her, and she reacted with a blind savagery of her own, lashing out at him with her tongue to silence him once and for all.

'He is dead! He caused all the harm that he could do many years ago. I am not superstitious! I simply do not want any part of anything that was my father's!'

'Then we will sleep in the open, Sara,' he said quietly, hearing the edge of hysteria in her voice. 'I will give them an explanation and they will be content, as you have made a decision that they wanted badly. I will light a fire and we will get whatever rest we can.' He reached for the main pack that he was carrying on Ronaldo, taking down too the rifle that he had so far ignored, and her eyes opened wide at the sight of this precaution.

'Animals,' he said caustically, 'not hostiles!'

Later, in the dark, when they were lying beside a fire that Jaime kept carefully alive, he turned his face to her and then, seeing that she was awake, he sat up. They had not in any way prepared for bed. Jaime was constantly replenishing the fire, and Sara had simply rolled herself as she was into the blankets. She was tired, but sleep would not come.

'What will you do now?' he asked quietly.

'I don't know,' she said dully. 'I promised my mother that I would never accept a penny from my grandmother. She hurt my mother so very much. It was a vow I made to my mother when she was dying. Now that he—my father is dead, the whole of the money comes to me.' She stared unseeingly at the night sky, at the wild, high stars. 'I have to keep that vow. Somehow, I've got to get rid of that money!' she finished desperately.

She heard his sharp intake of breath.

'You were wanting to find him to make sure that you got *nothing*?'

He sounded stunned and she smiled bitterly, sitting up and gazing into the firelight.

'Oh, yes. It almost cost me my life, but the vow was made and I agreed with it so much that nothing could have stopped me from coming to Mexico. He left us with that wicked old woman. He left us to cope with life in a place where my mother was hated and despised. Fifteen years! I remember you saying that. It was twenty years! Twenty years that turned my mother into an old woman and finally killed her. No, I don't want to take him home. He *is* home!'

CHAPTER TEN

IN SPITE of a near-sleepless night, when she had simply tossed restlessly and thought a great deal about her life in England, Sara felt no tiredness on the return journey. She was too tight inside, too deeply unhappy to relax enough to admit to tiredness.

Jaime was silent. From time to time she had found his eyes on her as she had turned uneasily in her bed, and he frequently turned his head to look at her as they made their way back along the pass to begin their descent to the village of Father Ovando. Perhaps he felt that she might fall asleep on Pepita's back and go the way of her nightdress, into the yawning spaces that edged the track. Or perhaps he was still stunned at her revelation and her bitterness. She did not know.

What she did know was that she would have to leave Mexico as soon as possible, and get back to England. She had an almost aching desire to see William, to talk to him and share her burden, and she knew that Jaime realised that they were very close to the end of their association, bitter-sweet as it had been.

They arrived early in the small village where Father Ovando lived, the sun only just beginning to set over the mountain peaks, and Sara took the opportunity to have a makeshift bath while Jaime bathed at the priest's house, telling him no doubt about the end of their search. Father Ovando's kindness at dinner was almost too much for Sara, and she was glad to have the small hut to herself as Jaime stayed at the Father's house and talked until late.

She was still awake, however, when he came to bed, and she kept her eyes tightly closed as he stood for a moment, looking down at her. The room was plunged into darkness as he put out the oil lamp, and then she heard him undress and get into his own bed.

The darkness was her undoing, because the pictures in her mind now flooded forward and swamped her, remorse eating away at her as she thought of the man who have never been to see her since she was a small child. She had never known him, never known how he felt, would never understand. Tears welled up inside, bringing soft, unhappy sounds from her that she stifled in the pillow as her slender body was racked with sobs.

'Sara?' Jaime's voice was soft in the darkness, and she tried hard to pull herself together.

'I—I'm all right.' Evidently he did not think so, because she heard his movements as he reached out to light the lamp that was on the small table close to his bed.

'Tell me,' he offered as the lamplight once again flooded the room. He was resting on his elbow, the blankets exposing bare chest, his dark eyes intently watching her face.

'I was thinking about my father,' she confessed in a whisper, avoiding his eyes. 'I was ... How could he leave us like that?' she suddenly burst out passionately. 'We were unhappy, poor! My mother was ill!' She turned to look at him, her eyes brimming with tears. 'Yet he was alone, too! I can't go on feeling bitter about a lonely old man.'

'He was not lonely, Sara,' he assured her softly. 'Do not fill you heart with more grief. There is a madness that sometimes comes over men, like a fever for gold. He would have always meant to come back to you, but time goes by and is easily lost. Another place to excavate, another clue to follow. Suddenly the years are gone and there is no going back. Suddenly, loved ones are strangers. I doubt if he simply deserted you in favour of old ruins. It was his job, the thing that he did always, and the distance was so great. After a while it would have become his only reality, to await every day for the great find, the hidden secrets of the past that he and only he could uncover. It is a madness, not a loneliness.'

She looked at him in the lamplight, some of the burden lifting from her heart, and his dark eyes looked back, hypnotic, calling to her.

'I was so bitter. I've been bitter for so long. Do you think that he knows, Jaime?'

Her eyes were filled with self-reproach, and he turned back the sheets of his bed, the lamplight gleaming on the brown, smooth skin of his waist, on the hard muscles of his chest. He held out his hand, the strong brown hand that had shaken her and caressed her.

'Come to me, Sara,' he said quietly, and she went to him with no hesitation. The spare shirt he had given her to replace her nightdress came to her thighs, the sleeves rolled up, the buttons fastened demurely, and as she lifted her slender legs from the bed to go to him, his dark eyes softened and smiled.

She slid into the warmth of his bed, unembarrassed to feel the strength of his legs against her own, already knowing that he was naked. She needed him, needed to be close to him, and he stayed resting on his arm, looking down into her eyes as he drew the blankets over her.

'Do you think that he knew how I felt, Jaime? Do you think that he knows now? I didn't even want to bring him back!'

'He is at peace, Sara,' he murmured softly. 'He is where he wished to be. I think that he knows now that you have no bitterness. The bitterness has gone, has it not, *pequeña*?'

'Yes.' She sighed deeply, knowing that it was true. She could not sustain the bitterness any longer, not now that she understood.

'They are all at peace, Sara,' he said quietly, his dark eyes searching her face. 'And you too must be at peace. You have done all that you could to keep your vow. It is over.'

His hands moved gently over her face, tracing her profile, smoothing back the bright hair, and she began to drift into the enchantment that she felt whenever he was near to her.

'What shall I do though about the money? I can't keep it.'

'It is a problem that can be solved without too much difficulty, *querida*,' he murmured. 'Tomorrow, we will think about it.'

'But, Jaime...'

'I will solve all your problems tomorrow, my beautiful Sara,' he soothed, his arms tightening around her. 'Tonight you must sleep.'

Sara made a small sound of protest, wanting to talk to him, wanting to tell him everything he did not know, but she was so tired. He was warm, comforting, easing her burden away, and she closed her eyes as he drew her close. Tomorrow. Tomorrow she would tell him. His stroking hand on her hair lulled her, and in a daze of enchantment she drifted into a deep sleep, safe in his arms.

Jaime's lips brushing her face awakened her in the early light of the morning, and she opened her eyes at once, knowing exactly where she was, not at all disoriented.

'So quick! So alert!' he mocked softly. 'Like a deer in the forest who awakes scenting danger. Do you scent danger, beautiful Sara?'

She shook her head, smiling into his eyes. She felt no danger with him now. She had lived for these days with him, alone in the mountains—the sky, the high peaks and Jaime her only world. They were close, attuned to each other, she had slept safely in his arms. There was nothing to fear with Jaime there.

'I'm not afraid,' she told him softly.

She stretched, languorous and warm, her silken legs brushing against his, and his eyes flared over her, light deep in the dark depths.

'I want you, Sara,' he said slowly. 'Perhaps there is something in that statement that will frighten you into flight.'

'I want you too, Jaime,' she whispered, looking up into his heavy, unsmiling eyes, 'and it doesn't frighten me.'

His fingers moved to the buttons of the blue shirt, slowly unfastening them as he looked down at her, his eyes on the silken swell of her breasts. He drew the shirt away, his hands caressing the smooth skin of her stomach.

'*Dios!* You are beautiful!' he murmured, smokily soft. 'You are as beautiful as I knew you would be!'

She felt beautiful, wanted to be for Jaime, and no thought of past or future entered her head. There was only the glorious wonder of being here with him at last.

His dark head bent to her breast, his mouth warm and compelling on the sharp, rosy nipple, and she sighed in wonder, turning into his arms, delighting in the warm contact with his hard, strong body, softening against him as he lifted her to fit her closely to his powerful, masculine frame.

'At last! To own you, to feel you melt in my arms, become a part of me,' he whispered huskily. 'If I do not possess you, my life will be forever incomplete!'

His hands came to her full breasts, stroking over the hardened nipples gently and expertly until she was lost in need, her whole body on fire. His lips came down fiercely on hers as his hands continued to stroke her, to explore her body with a raging desire, and she clung to him blindly, offering herself completely to this dark, powerful man who had forced his way into her life.

Teasing and nipping, his mouth moved over her until the very breath seemed to be drawn from her body, and she leapt with excitement, her breath a gasp in her throat!

'Jaime!' Small whimpers of desire came from her lips as she twisted urgently against him; longing sounds that had him claiming her mouth, his lips leaving their intimate exploration of her body as he moved fully over her, lifting her close.

'I know, *cariña*,' he murmured soothingly, his breathing hard and fast. 'We are like two souls in torment. Together we will reach heaven!'

Desire raged through her. She was molten in his arms, and he acknowledged his own need with a deep groan as his lips fused with hers.

'Dear God! I want you so badly! It is a hunger that will never end! With you I am willing to forget honour, promises, anything!'

His caresses made her body jerk with delight, and she found herself murmuring against his skin, her tongue testing the salty smoothness of his neck and shoulders.

'Please! Jaime!' She begged for his possession, and his voice was almost unrecognisable as he murmured to her words in his own language that she did not understand. But she understood the need in him that soared to match her own, and she understood the things that he was trying to say.

He framed her face with his hands, his mouth compelling on hers, druggingly sweet, sending her soaring into the same blind passion that engulfed him, and when he lifted her to fit her to his hard and powerful body she came willingly and wildly, needing no urging to belong to him.

Pain, fierce, and unbelievable, hit her at the powerful thrust of his possession, and there was no way that she could prevent the gasp of shock that left her lips. She was aware of the startled look in his burning, dark eyes, the momentary rejection that shuddered through him, and then he gathered her back to him with a strength and gentleness that relit all the fires that her pain had doused.

'Sara!' He groaned her name as the full weight of his body crushed hers, and sweet liquid honey seemed to fill her entire being as, with a tenderness that she found breathtaking and arousing, he led her to the very peak of desire and beyond.

For a time afterwards, he lay against her, his breathing unsteady, only moving when she eased her cramped limbs languidly. She belonged to him! The pain was forgotten, happiness was soaring inside her, and nothing mattered but Jaime and her love for him.

He moved from her and stood with one swift movement, dressing in angry silence, his tall, lean frame tight with disapproval as he turned back to her with cold and glistening eyes.

'Why did you not tell me?' He was looking at her with such fury that she shuddered, and he flicked the covers over her naked body with an impatient gesture.

'Jaime, I...' Her gentle protest only seemed to infuriate him more, and he towered over her, his eyes blazing with anger.

'You are living with a man, with this—William!' he groaned out bitterly. 'It had never occurred to me that you may be a virgin, that you have some peculiar arrangement with this man whereby he is content to not lay a hand on you. He must be a saint! You were saving this prize until you could both be married? Was it beyond you to have told me?'

'Jaime! You don't understand! I'm not going to marry William!'

He stopped her before she could explain further, his movements impatients and angry.

'You are not, and that is true. In my country, a man does not take a girl's virginity lightly! It is a matter of honour, and if no honour exists, then her father and brothers are quite prepared to take up weapons if necessary. I have robbed you of your virtue. Naturally you will marry me as soon as it can be arranged!'

There was no love in him, that was very clear. There was no tenderness, none of the sweet and wonderful feeling that had flooded through her before his harsh voice had chilled it from her. He had thought that she was sleeping with another man, but he had wanted her sufficiently to make love to her anyway.

Now his pride and honour were injured, and he was demanding marriage with an arrogant expectation of her acceptance, all simply to heal the wound to his pride. He had no thought for her whatsoever. She had been just a girl who was more than willing.

She accepted the deep thrust of pain with a pale, blank face, her blue eyes devoid of feeling. All her feelings were inside—grief and humiliation choking her. She could not react in any other way than with coldness, because to have shown emotion would have been the end of her.

'I have no intention of marrying you to salve your conscience,' she told him bitterly and coldly. 'You already know that I have a very poor opinion of your country. Be easy in your mind, though. I wanted to make love just as much as you did. It doesn't change the way I think, however. I hadn't realised until I met you that a woman can feel exactly the same sort of desire as a man, a desire with nothing whatever behind it. It does not alter any of my feelings for William. To go with you and leave him would be the end of me, and I have a great instinct for self-preservation!'

He stared at her with narrowed eyes, his hands clenched and his face tight, and then he turned away abruptly.

'Yes!' he said in a taut, angry voice. 'There is William, the constant and the faithful! I did say once, *señorita*, that one day we may forget William! The day has arrived! I cannot force you into marriage, even to satisfy my own honour!'

Sara wanted to cry out her love for him, but surely he must know? He had not said any word of love to her except the soft and soothing words that any man might say to a woman when his passion was aroused.

María-Teresa was his future, and he had been prepared to sacrifice that. What would her life be then? She would be a constant reminder to him of all he had given up for one moment of passion. And he had made a vow to his father. Sara knew all about vows made to a parent. There was also the call of the untamed land, the distant mountains. There was nothing that she would ever say to tie him to a life he would not want; she loved him too much for that.

'I will bring water for you to wash!' he said tightly. 'If you are not too exhausted, we will leave at once. There is a long way to go, but I think that if we keep moving steadily, we may well be able to miss out our overnight stop at the *rancho* and make it to the house by midnight.'

'But—but you never travel at night. You told me so when...'

'Normally, no, but I am prepared to take the chance tonight. Tomorrow, I expect, you will wish to go home.'

'Home?' Her deep blue eyes accused him, and he turned away impatiently.

'Yes, home!' he ground out savagely. 'You have commitments in your own country, do you not?' He turned back to her when she did not answer. 'Well?' he exclaimed sharply.

She looked away, her eyes refusing to meet his. Yes, she had commitments; money to get rid of and a cousin who would need her. Certainly Jaime did not need her. The man who had held her close all night, who had loved her so recently, no longer existed.

'Answer me!' he grated, and she lifted her head, meeting his eyes without a tremor, shuttering the love that would have shone out of them.

'Yes, I have commitments,' she managed in an even voice that was a masterpiece of acting. 'I have a fortune to squander, and then, of course, there's William.'

He drew in his breath harshly, his face tightening to dark anger. 'Yes, he said savagely. 'There is William!'

He walked out and left her to get ready, and she did not attempt to enlighten him about her cousin William, who was all the family she had, who was bright, cheerful and faithful. Let him imagine that William was simply a man she loved, a man she lived with, as she remembered once telling him to annoy him. She would never cling and trap the man she loved. She knew where his love rested. He was, in his own way, like her father, constantly seeking the distant mountains. He must be free to follow his heart and fulfil his vows.

It was Hernando who took her to the plane and flew her out of Jaime's life. Jaime, with meticulous care, had made reservations for her in Mexico City, booked her seat on a plane to England and then he had gone. All she had wanted to do was to leave also, but she did not get free without a little advice from Constanza Carreras.

'I am pleased that you are not attempting to stay here now that your search is over, Señorita Lawrence,' she had said, coming into Sara's room as she packed to leave. 'I know that it is easy to become attached to someone like Jaime, especially considering the pitiful condition that you were in when you arrived. He is kindness itself, but he is not a man to break his vows. I have already told you that when María-Teresa is old enough, they will marry.'

Yes, she had already told her, and now she was rubbing it in to make quite sure, salt into a raw wound. Sara said nothing, though. It was pointless. Jaime was gone, and now she too would go and never see this place, this country again.

She told Hernando of Constanza's words as he flew her to the city, sitting beside him, completely unafraid of the flight. She had faced the worst thing that she would ever have to face. Jaime did not love her, and no aircraft, no mountain pass could equal the distress of that.

Hernando snorted with annoyance and glanced sharply at her pale face.

'I hope that you have not let her upset you, *señorita*,' he said forcefully. 'There is not one grain of truth in it. It is her own wishful thinking. The only vow that Jaime made to his father was to keep that woman here, to look after her and his stepsister, who was then very young. The *señora* is well provided for and has a grand house in the city, but she remains with Jaime in the hope that he will one day decide that he needs a wife and take the nearest girl available. She thinks that it will obviously be María-Teresa. It will not!'

'How can you be so sure?' Sara asked dully. 'María-Teresa seems to be content to simply stay at the house with all its isolation. Perhaps she wouldn't mind being left behind while Jaime disappears into the mountains.'

'She stays for me!' Hernando said sharply. 'We love each other!'

'Then why...' Sara was open-mouthed, but many of María-Teresa's jealous glances now could be explained, and also why Jaime's assertion that she would not welcome Sara. 'Why don't you marry her?'

'We have told no one,' he said with a shrug. 'You are the only one to have that honour, *señorita*!'

Sara was not so sure of that. The quiet conspiracy between Jaime and María-Teresa now took on other meanings.

'We must bide our time. The *señora* would never permit it. She is after bigger fish. Jaime is rich beyond her wildest dreams, and besides, I am not *criollo*. They are!'

He probably had an ally who was more powerful than the *señora*, Sara thought, one who proudly called himself a Mexican and cared not for such things as being *criollo* and tracing his descent from Spain itself. But it was not her place to tell Hernando. Jaime would see to their happiness, but he could not see to hers. He had not asked her to marry him because he loved her, only to salve his pride. It seemed now that he was not in any way tied to someone else, he just did not want her.

Hernando did not mention the family again until he was putting her into a taxi to get her to her hotel, then he leaned in at the window and gently touched her face.

'Why do you not simply turn around and go back to him, *señorita*?' he asked quietly, and she did not attempt to prevaricate.

'He doesn't love me,' she said softly, and he laughed quietly before waving her off.

'You are younger, I think, in your mind than María-Teresa. Also you are English. It is a big handicap.'

Five months later, the handicap remained. Her love for Jaime was as strong as ever, a deep, aching loneliness that would never pass. She stood at the upstairs window of the office in the large country house that she and William had bought with some of the legacy, and watched him as he made his way around the lawn, talking to the children who played there supervised by the trained staff.

At last, William's dreams were realised and, although there were still many things to do, he was doing what he had wanted to do for years, working with children who had not had the chance for the love that had been given to him as a boy. The legacy had made that possible. They had bought and altered the house, setting up a trust fund for the future of the home, and his happiness was now complete.

She watched him walking round the lawn, his footsteps never stumbling, but his stick ever-present. Her courageous and kindly William. Without him, she would not have survived these past few months. She saw him lift his head and then walk to the gate in the thick old hedge, his hand outstretched to greet someone, and her heart leapt into her throat at the sight of the tall, lean man who came forward, smiling.

His hair was black as night, his skin dark and tanned to a deep gold, his teeth white as snow against the dark, handsome face. Jaime! She turned away in distress, knowing that when she looked again he would be gone.

So many times she had seen him, seen him in every dark head, every handsome, smiling face, and always he had been a mirage. She turned back to look and he was not there. William was alone, talking to a child, a lame child who laughed up into his smiling face.

Misery, bleak and total, swept over her, and she sat down on the nearest chair, her body shaking with heart-broken sobs. How long was this going to continue? How long must she live like this? Now, Jaime would be in the mountains or in his office in Mexico City, no thought of her in his mind.

There was a sharp knock on the door and she hastily tried to dry her eyes. William must have seen her at the window; he missed nothing, and her misery would only upset him. It had upset him when she had returned to England and poured out her heart to him.

'One moment!' Her call was ignored, however, and she heard the door open. 'Oh, William! I'm perfectly all right!'

She dried her eyes and turned, stopping in white-faced shock to see Jaime standing in the doorway, his dark eyes intent on her distressed face.

'I didn't say, "Come in"!' she said defensively, standing shakily to face him. There was a wild look in her eyes, utter disbelief that he was actually standing there, almost close enough to touch.

'I did not wait to hear it,' he answered coolly, walking further into the room. 'I imagined that you would want to see me before I left the place.'

'I—what are you doing here? How did you know...'

'Your cousin William wrote to me,' he said evenly, ignoring her tear-stained face and sitting on the edge of her desk. 'He wanted to thank me for caring for you after your accident. He also wanted to thank me for my help in your search for your father. I was in England, and so I thought that I would call to see him.'

'Oh. It—it was very nice of you. William never told me that...'

'It was not very nice of me,' he interrupted, his dark eyes on her face. 'I wanted to see if he was telling the truth when he said you were unhappy.' His glittering black glaze flared over her body. 'You are too thin, more fragile than ever! Is this how William takes care of you?'

He was angry, domineering, his whole body stiff with some carefully suppressed emotion that could only be rage, and she shook her head in confusion, unable to understand his attitude or the reason for his coming, frightened when he suddenly stood and moved closer.

'You are afraid of me?' he asked softly. 'I have snatched you from the gods, led you over the mountains, allowed you to leave Mexico, and now you are afraid?'

'I'm not afraid,' she managed, looking away from the dark, hypnotic eyes. 'I—I'm just surprised, that's all. You—you've caught me off balance.'

'I have caught you weeping!' he asserted steadily. 'You fled from Mexico to return to your William, and now you weep. You are still not at peace.'

'I am! Really, I am!' She bit her lips anxiously, her eyes avoiding his. 'We've done everything that we set out to do, William and I. This is just the place that he had planned. You can see how well things are going.'

She glanced up, but his dark eyes were expressionless, and she had the feeling that he was simply allowing her to run on blindly, giving her enough rope with which to hang herself, to talk herself into trouble.

'You can see that William needs me,' she said quickly. 'You must have noticed that he's lame. We—we set up this home with the legacy,' she managed a quick, uneasy smile, 'so you see, you were quite right. It's not a problem, after all. I mean, everything's all right now...'

'He does not need you, Sara!' he said harshly, ignoring everything else she had rushed on to say. 'He is a contented man. His dream is realised, as he told me in his letter. You are clinging to someone who does not need you in the slightest, except perhaps as a well-loved relative. You are destroying yourself in the same way that you were destroying yourself with guilt about the money.'

'He does need me!' Her hands came to her hot and tear-stained face. 'How can you say that? You don't know me at all really, and you don't know what William needs.'

'I know that you are passionate, and likely to tear yourself apart with ideas of loyalty, justice and guilt! Also, do not speak to me about knowing you.' He took a step forward, bringing him dangerously close. 'I know you! And I am well able to assess need, I have plenty of my own to contemplate!'

'You don't need me,' she whispered, her hands now twisting together. 'You want to be free, to live your life as you've chosen. You want to roam the mountains and all the empty places.'

He moved quickly, as smoothly and fast as a great cat, pulling her roughly into his arms to look down into the deep, unhappy blue of her eyes.

'You little fool! There is an empty place in my life without you, and an empty place in my heart that no one else will ever fill.' He stared down at her aggressively, holding her tightly, and then suddenly cradled her against him, his voice softening to the smoky tenderness she had heard the night in the mountains when he had claimed her as his own. 'Tell me that you love me! Tell me that you will go back with me, back to Mexico. I will not be separated from you again.' He pulled back and looked down at her, his eyes narrowed. 'You have

used William as a shield against me and, fool that I am,
I believed it all. I was even too jealous to let you explain,
although now I realise that you tried to, several times.
When he wrote to me, I was very angry with you. I
thought that you still would not come to me, even though
you knew that there was nothing to keep us apart!' His
dark eyes began to smile, and he cupped her head in his
hand. 'All that I could hope for was that you were
pregnant and that was the cause of your unhappiness.'

She pulled away to stare at him, disbelief in her face.

'Hope for? You wanted me to—to be pregnant?'

'I longed for it! I want you with me, in any way that
I can get you!' He rocked her gently. 'But alas, I can
see that it is not true. You are merely unhappy. You are
not going to come to me, Sara?' he questioned softly.
'You are not going to admit that you love me?'

'I didn't know...I thought...' She was suddenly sure,
filled with a blaze of happiness, and she wound her arms
around his neck, clinging to him fiercely. 'Oh, Jaime! I
love you so much! I thought you didn't love me! I
thought you wanted to be free, like my father!'

'And I thought that William was the man you wanted,
although you gave yourself to me.' He looked down at
her, his hand cupping her face, his arm tightly around
her. 'Ah, *querida*! I had held you in my arms all the
long night, and then loved you with every fibre of my
being. I was wildly angry that I had taken your inno-
cence, shocked that every last thing I had thought about
you was untrue. I could not even begin to hope that you
loved me. I had been so savage to you, berated you for
greed, for staying here with a man who was not your
husband. I wanted you enough to try and take you away
from him, to marry you and keep you for ever. I was
horrified and guilty, and I blazed into anger against you.'

He looked down at her ruefully.

'What could I have expected except that you would blaze back at me? You said words that burned themselves on to my heart, and I had to let you go.'

'I never wanted anyone but you!' Sara cried, her hand coming to stroke the dark face that was so very dear to her. 'Even when I saw you in London, and you were so horrid to me, I couldn't forget you.'

'Nor I you, *querida*,' he smiled, sitting and taking her on his lap. 'When I saw you in the forest, I knew that if I could snatch you away from the gods, I would never let you go!'

'You did!' Sara reminded him, and he traced her soft lips with his brown finger.

'Only because I imagined that you wanted to go,' he assured her. 'Do not try to leave me again, or you will be shocked at my primitive reaction!'

'You'll leave me,' she reminded him quietly. 'You'll need to go into the mountains to be alone.'

'I have never gone there to be alone,' he said firmly. 'I have only gone to serve my people. Now, either someone else can go, or you will go with me as you went before.' He smiled into her eyes. 'Did it not occur to you, *mi amor*, that I could easily have flown you to the Indian village by helicopter? We are not a backward country. Such machines are known to us, you understand?'

'Then why...' She looked into his eyes wonderingly, and he kissed her gently, a smile softening the hard lines of his handsome face.

'I wanted the time to last,' he confessed softly. 'I wanted to be alone with you, to give you room to think. I prayed that you would love me and never wish to leave. Every day, I watched you for some sign that you cared, and I thought that you did. I would never have made love to you if I had not been sure.' He smiled into her eyes as she blushed deeply. 'Ah, you are shy with me. That means that you have not been loved enough.' He suddenly stood, putting her on her feet and glancing round impatiently.

'Come!' he ordered in his old arrogant manner. 'We cannot stay here, and I do not intend to spend my day bowing to William's sensibilities. Pack the things that you will need for tonight. Tomorrow we will get the rest.'

'But I can't leave William—just like that!' She pulled fretfully at the hard hand that she had thought would never be on her arm again. She was confused by his determination, and anxious, wanting to cling to him but frightened that he would hurt her again. 'I can't just walk out!'

'William is a big boy now!' he said emphatically. 'And if you do not care for my hand on your arm, I will carry you out! I suspect that your William would be delighted with that. He has a smile that lives deep in his eyes.'

'He'd never stop laughing,' Sara admitted with a faint smile of her own. 'Where are we going, though?'

'I have a very nice, cosy room in a hotel a few miles away,' he said with a smile that had her cheeks flushing. 'We are going to stay there together.'

'I thought that you didn't take such things lightly in your country?' she reminded him breathlessly, her anxiety and confusion bringing an amused gleam to his glittering eyes.

'We do not! But then, *cariña*, I intend to marry you three times. Once in your own church, once a civil ceremony because it is not my religion, and once again in Mexico, just to make sure!'

'Oh, Jaime!' she laughed, flying into his arms. 'Once will be enough!'

'No!' he said determinedly, gathering her close. 'I intend to take no chance!'

* * *

Not too long afterwards, wrapped in the security of Jaime's arm, Sara voiced a worrying thought.

'What about Señora Carreras and María-Teresa?' The thought of going back to the annoyed looks of Jaime's stepmother marred her happiness, but he turned her face up to his as she lay contentedly in his embrace.

'The only Señora Carreras will be you! As to Constanza, she has decided that the bright lights of Mexico City are very attractive, and my promise to my father is at an end.'

'Hernando told me about that,' she said softly, and he looked down at her arrogantly.

'Si! He has driven me to great anger, constantly advising me to bring you back. He is not now my secretary!'

'You dismissed him? You monster!'

Her annoyance turned to small squeals of laughter as his teeth nipped her bare shoulder.

'You will remember who is the master, my little wretch!' he threatened with a smile that robbed his words of any threat at all. 'And I have not dismissed him! He is promoted to the city as my personal representative. Next month, he is to marry María-Teresa. She finally told her mother the truth, and insisted on her freedom from maternal domination. I told Constanza that if I could not have you, then there would be nobody else, and I used my influence. She is slightly mollified by Hernando's promotion, so all goes well.'

'Hernando is not *criollo*,' Sara reminded him softly, her finger tracing his lips.

'He is Mexican!' Jaime said showing where his pride lay. 'In any case, *mi amor*, you are not *criollo* either, and I will marry you, though all the gods in creation attempt to stop me!'

'Jaime,' she suddenly said softly. 'Why were you so adamant that I shouldn't see my father?'

For a moment, he looked down at her seriously, and then signed deeply, moving to the side and taking her in his arms.

'Will you always ask the questions that I would rather not answer, my love?' he asked gently. 'I knew what had happened to your father. Oh, I did not know that he was dead. It was several years since he had been heard of, and no one was sure, but those of use who knew the mountains knew also that your father had given up any attempt to resist the pull of the place. I tried to tell you when you were in London, but I could not bring myself to do it. I could not bear to think of the look on your face.

'Your father thought of himself as an Indian, seemed to remember nothing else. The last time that I saw him, I spoke to him in his own language and he did not even understand. He seemed to be happy, and I knew how long it had been since he was in his own country. It did not occur to me that he had a daughter. The Indians cared for him, worshipped him and, as I say, he was happy. I left him to live out his life in peace.'

'Oh, Jaime!' Sara's blue eyes filled with tears, and he tightened his arms around her.

'Do not weep for him, *mi amor*,' he said tenderly. 'He was happy, and through him we have found each other. Now he knows and will be happier still.'

She nodded, her mind eased by this gentle philosophy, her eyes smiling into his when he looked down at her worriedly, his anxiety easing when she wound her arms around his neck and kissed his cheek.

'You will have to do better than that, *querida*!' he threatened softly, his lips hovering over hers, but she had not finished yet.

'Why did you hate me as soon as you saw me?' she asked tremulously.

'Hate you?' He threw his head back and laughed. 'I looked across the room and saw you, a girl who had stepped straight out of my dreams. I was stunned, could not believe it, and I was also furious with myself when I realised that I wanted to walk across, unannounced, and take you into my arms! It is an unnerving thing, my darling, to meet your fate without warning.'

'You were absolutely horrid to me!' she said angrily, her face flushing when she remembered how her breath had stopped at the sight of him.

'One needs room for manoeuvre!' he said arrogantly. 'I had not decided how I was going to get you for myself. For once, you had me at a disadvantage!'

'But you believed so many bad things about me!' she reminded him. 'How could you want me for yourself when you thought I was a person like that?'

'I wanted you for myself from the moment that I first saw you,' he said quietly. 'What I thought you were did not seem to matter. I could not forget you because I loved you. Then, when I heard that you were in Mexico, intent on flying out to find your father, I was determined that nobody else would take you over the mountains. I was determined to meet you and shake some sense into you if need be, but you crashed!' He tightened his arms around her. 'Ah, *querida*! I thought that you would be dead, that I would never again look into those deep blue eyes, that they would never smile for me.' He kissed her lingeringly, his arms a shelter from all trouble. 'When I found you alive, I vowed to keep you, to take you from William.'

They lay silently, looking into each other's eyes and he smiled softly.

'Do we love each other, *dulce amor*?' he asked softly, and she kissed his smiling lips, murmuring her love over and over again.

'It is not every day, *querida*, that a man's prayers are answered,' he sighed contentedly, his lips trailing kisses down the length of her slender neck.

She could not resist the temptation to ask another question. 'What about María-Teresa, Jaime? You were very close to her. I thought you loved her.' She was very quiet, very serious, and he smiled wickedly.

'I have taken care of her since she was a small girl, *querida*,' he said. 'I know her well. She is jealous of her possessions and counted me as one of them. Though she loves Hernando, she still clung to me like a child. I hid behind that possessiveness, not willing to tell you how I felt, knowing that you hated me roundly.'

'I thought I did!' Sara said wonderingly, and he laughed delightedly, moving slowly, coming over her with quiet deliberation, amusement in his dark, dancing eyes.

'Sometimes you will hate me,' he said softly, his eyes on her smiling lips. 'It is the way we will be, fighting and loving. But it will never be dull, *mi amor*, and when the final word is spoken, it will be one of love. You are much given to questioning everything. I will have to put a stop to that. You have always talked yourself into trouble, since the moment that I first met you. All you need to say from now on is yes!'

He looked down at her, and her happiness soared at the love and desire that she saw in his eyes.

'Well, *querida*?' he asked softly.

'Yes, Jaime,' she whispered, her eyes closing in contentment as his lips covered hers.

Harlequin Presents

Coming Next Month

1199 THE ALOHA BRIDE Emma Darcy
Robyn is at a low point in her life and is determined not to be hurt again. Then she meets Julian Lassiter Somehow she finds herself wanting to solve Julian's problems in a way that is not only reckless but is positively dangerous!

1200 FANTASY LOVER Sally Heywood
Torrin Anthony's arrival in Merril's life is unwanted and upsetting, for this shallow, artificial actor reminds her of Azur—the heroic rebel sympathizer who'd rescued her from cross fire in the Middle East. Could she possibly be mixing fantasy with reality?

1201 WITHOUT TRUST Penny Jordan
Lark Cummings, on trial for crimes she's innocent of, hasn't a chance when she is faced with James Wolfe's relentless prosecution. Then the case is inexplicably dropped. She wants to hate this formidable man, but finds it impossible when fate brings him back into her life!

1202 DESPERATION Charlotte Lamb
Megan accepts a year apart from her newfound love, Devlin Hurst—she'll wait for him. Yet when her life turns upside down just hours after his departure, she knows she must break their pact. Only she has to lie to do it...

1203 TAKE AWAY THE PRIDE Emma Richmond
Toby lies about her qualifications to become secretary to powerful Marcus du Mann—and is a disaster. But when Marcus gets stuck with his baby nephew, Toby is put in charge. And she's coping well—until Marcus decides to move in and help...

1204 TOKYO TRYST Kay Thorpe
Two years ago, Alex walked out on Greg Wilde when she discovered he was unfaithful. Now they're on the same work assignment in Japan. Despite Greg's obvious interest in the beautiful Yuki, Alex finds herself falling in love with him all over again!

1205 IMPULSIVE GAMBLE Lynn Turner
Free-lance journalist Abbie desperately wants a story on reclusive engineer-inventor Malacchi Garrett. Then she discovers the only way to get close to him is by living a lie. But how can she lie to the man she's falling in love with?

1206 NO GENTLE LOVING Sara Wood
Hostile suspicion from wealthy Dimitri Kastelli meets Helen in Crete, where she's come to find out about the mother she never knew. What grudge could he hold against a long-dead peasant woman? And how would he react if he learned who Helen is?

Available in September wherever paperback books are sold, or through Harlequin Reader Service:

In the U.S.
901 Fuhrmann Blvd.
P.O. Box 1397
Buffalo, N.Y. 14240-1397

In Canada
P.O. Box 603
Fort Erie, Ontario
L2A 5X3